A DEBUT NOVEL

BY

DESI STOWE

Dedication

To those of you in healthcare who have walked down hospital hallways and slipped unnoticed into empty stairwells, if only for a moment, to deal with the tirade of emotions that come from serving others, I see you.

I see your silent tears for the patient you couldn't save.

I see you as you compassionately care for others while neglecting the care you need.

I see your fear when serving those who threaten violence.

I see your rage at the injustice life can bring.

I see your exhaustion from being overworked.

I see your struggles from being underpaid.

This book is dedicated to you.

Your service to others is not unnoticed.

It's the wee hours of a warm, early spring morning when I finally arrive home after catching the last red-eye flight available. Getting out of Chicago was an absolute necessity, even if I did have to fly in the middle of the night. I stumble into bed fully dressed, surrendering to the exhaustion that's been chasing me for weeks. I awaken hours later by the deep rumbling thunder of a late morning storm.

Clumsily, I reach for my phone to check the time when I see I have four voicemails. *Fantastic.* Why the people in my life insist on calling and won't text like normal human beings I'll never know.

Vivian, you promised me you'd be my date for the charity gala. We had a deal! I want to see you back in Chicago by tonight ...

Yeah… that's not happening, Fitzgerald.

Delete.

Vivian! I'm so glad you are home!! Dinner tonight at our favorite taco place? Love you, Sis...

Dinner sounds great. I would love to see my sister and who doesn't want to eat tacos?!?

Viv, it's Hal. Fitzgerald is not happy. You can't keep doing this, you gotta play the game.

I know what game Chad Fitzgerald wants to play. *No thanks.*

Delete.

Viv, it's Hal again. I need you in New York in 48 hours. Quick turnaround this time.

I audibly groan, though no one's around to offer sympathy. It's exactly the news I do NOT want to hear. I just finished a successful, albeit intense, assignment at WindyCity Robotics, complete with a salary bonus and what was supposed to be a full week off. I consider myself quite career-driven, but somewhere in the deep recesses of my mind, I understand this pace is not sustainable.
I've been working at least 12 hours a day, every day, for the past two months. When I'm working, I have zero downtime.

I work weekends and holidays. The hours are brutally long. I was looking forward to having more time than a weekend to recuperate. I stretch, my muscles ache, and protest the movement. My body is struggling but my mind starts racing. I need to get moving if I need to be in New York in a couple of days.

Ungracefully, I fall out of bed. Mornings have never been my strong suit. I stagger into the kitchen so I can fuel up on caffeine and find some coherence of thought. My cabinets are bare, but I won't be here long enough for a grocery store run. I rummage around in my bag and find a granola bar for breakfast. Not quite ready to speak to other humans yet, I text my sister to confirm dinner plans for the evening.

I grab my notebook and a favorite pen and start making an updated game plan. I look at the to-do list I created yesterday when I thought I had a week off and frown. I need to adjust to fit things into the shortened timeline. I make three columns: one to prioritize the absolute must-do items, one for the maybes, and the last column is full of the items that will unfortunately not happen. Now that I only have a couple of days, I'll be mostly running the inevitable errands of adulthood. *So much for the day at the spa.*

I spend most of the day checking off my to-do list and then stopping for a much-needed shower before I meet my sister for dinner. I change into a tee shirt, jeans, and sneakers - the exact opposite of my usual business suit and heels.

I arrive at the restaurant and wrap my arms around my older sister, Lily. She beams at me and pulls me in for another hug. We walk arm in arm to the table where her husband Jonathon is already waiting, along with her friend, Oliver. I glare at my sister, who only gives me a sweet smile as she sits down. I like Oliver, we've been casual friends for a few years. He went to college with Lily and her husband. I'm not disappointed to see him at all. I am, however, annoyed at Lily for her continual match-making efforts. She has it in her head that if I found "Mr. Right" I'd settle down and not travel so much. It's hard to be too angry with her. She only wants me around more.

Fortunately, Oliver knows my sister well and isn't fooled by her schemes. I hug him and he quickly whispers, "I know what they're playing at and I would've said no. But you know I have a weakness for tacos."

I laugh, I can't help it. Oliver has a weakness for food in general. I pull away from the hug and smile up at him. "Well, you are in luck, my friend. Tacos are my treat tonight!"

"Sweet!!!" He gives me a high five and we find seats. As we sit down Oliver says, "So I gather business is good?"

"Yeah, I had a successful assignment working with WindyCity Robotics. I was able to recruit back a couple of the top talents they had lost to competitors. I also worked on creating a better work environment so they don't continue to lose personnel."

Lily asks, "WindyCity Robotics? Who are they? I've never heard of them."

"No one has! Their marketing department needs some serious work. But I just focused on personnel issues." The conversation pauses while our waitress drops off chips and salsa.

My brother-in-law Jonathon typically does not join in the conversation much when Lily and I are together. *Probably because he can't get a word in edgewise.* But today he's chatty and adds, "I haven't heard of them either. It costs so much to hire and train new people. It's just good business sense to focus efforts on employee retention. I feel like a lot of companies don't get that. It's good to hear they were receptive to that message."

Turning to Lily, I say, "I like my brother-in-law. Keep him around, yeah?"

She rolls her eyes. "I plan on keeping him around. I'd like to keep you around too."

I cringe. "I'm back in New York in a couple of days. Then, who knows?"

Lily protests, "I thought you had a week off!"

I rub her back to give her some comfort. I realize this news is more disappointing to her than it is to me. "I know me too. Something came up that's urgent - I won't know the details until I get to New York."

Oliver has been busy inhaling chips and salsa but stops at my statement. "Could your boss send you to Seattle? I've always wanted to go there. I'll come to visit you if he does."

I shrug. "I've not been to the Pacific Northwest before, but it's a possibility."

Lily, who honestly just can't help herself, has to add, "You can visit her wherever she goes..."

Oliver ponders this for a moment and says, "No can do. If she goes further south I can't visit. The humidity is too much for my hair." We all laugh as Oliver styles his hair using the reflection of the back of his spoon.

After dinner, Oliver walks me to my car. "I know historically we've had the whole we're-married-to-our-work thing in common. Just thought you might want to know, I've met someone. Her name is Paige. She's busy working on her dissertation tonight; she's getting a PhD in genetics.

I stop to glance up at him. "Wow, that sounds impressive."

"I know! She's very smart, except for her taste in men." Oliver chuckles at his joke and then continues, "She knows I was here as part of a match-making scheme tonight. She also knows you and I have always been just friends, much to Lily's dismay."

"You are a gem, Paige is lucky to have you. You're going to break my sister's heart, you know. I think she's already drafted our wedding invitations," I tease.

Oliver laughs. "She is a bit much, but your sister loves you dearly. She misses you when you're gone."

We say our goodbyes. I'm genuinely happy for my friend. Just because I'm married to my work doesn't mean I expect that lifestyle from others. I know it's not the norm. My work is the quickest path to financial security, and that's my priority. I didn't have much money during college. I had to watch every dime I spent. I don't need fancy things, not really. I just want a padded savings account for my peace of mind. I HATE the stress that comes with being broke and living paycheck to paycheck.

I haven't given the idea of a long-term relationship much thought, other than it seems incompatible with my current lifestyle. It's not like I meet men I would be serious about anyway.

I had my phone off during dinner, so I take a moment to check my messages. Speaking of men I wouldn't be serious about, Chad Fitzgerald has called me again.

> *Hey, it's Chad. Again. I know when I've been ghosted. Just wanted to say I would have taken the job at WindyCity without you faking interest in me. I thought we had something real…*

I groan and delete the message early. I wish Chad would just be angry with me. That much I deserve, I wasn't all that fair to him. Instead of anger, which I could totally handle, he sounds sad. Sadness is a gateway to guilt. What's done is done, guilt would be an unwelcome guest in my thoughts.

I met Chad while I was in Chicago. He's a top talent in the robotics industry. WindyCity wanted him back desperately and paid me a hefty recruitment bonus to convince him to sign a contract. I pulled out all my usual techniques, but Chad was stubborn. WindyCity was not the only one courting him, either.

While I use flirtation to speed things along on any assignment, I went past my usual boundaries to recruit Chad. I did strongly lead him to believe romance was on the horizon. I promised to attend a charity gala with him while I was sitting on his lap. Chad's a decent guy. If he'd just been like my typical obnoxious clientele, I wouldn't give it a second thought. Chad's nice. Dorky, but in an adorable little brother kind of way.

The most irksome part was that if WindyCity had upped his salary offer a bit more, recruiting Chad would have been a breeze. I told Chad I never mix work and pleasure, which is true.

I let him think things would change as soon as I finished at his firm. I ended up making promises I had no intention of keeping just so I could finish in Chicago. *I desperately needed to escape the bitter cold unending winter.*

I ignore my other messages and whatever drama is contained therein, instead opting to go to bed early. I want to catch up on some much-needed rest. I block all thoughts of Chad Fitzgerald out of my head and fall into a quiet and dreamless sleep.

New York

A few years ago, my boss, Hal, took me under his wing as his protegé. Back in college, I was painfully shy and awkward. *So awkward.* What I lacked in social skills, however, I made up for in determination in academics. My presentation on workplace culture was sent to Aberlin Consulting. He hired me on the spot.

Hal taught me how to use small talk effectively, where I appeared to be genuinely interested in the person I spoke to. He educated me on how to read people and situations - to know when to walk away and when to close the deal. He set me up with a stylist who gave me a makeover and instructed me on how to use my appearance to my advantage. I may have started as a clueless university student, but I morphed into a professional consultant in a few short weeks.

I finally have an update on my next assignment and I've been given my biggest challenge yet. A healthcare system is hiring us for staff recruitment and retention.

Hospitals lost staff during the height of the pandemic, which is not terribly surprising. I guess some of those didn't have the grit to stick around. Even now though, workers keep leaving.

I arrive at my firm's office building in Manhattan. I'm wearing a business suit and heels, but I stashed my running gear in my bag. I'm close enough for a run through Central Park when I am done, which is just what I need to clear my head. Hal has few meetings, but when he does meet, it's an experience of information overload.

I'm a few minutes early and wait just outside Hal's office. I won't have to wait long. He's always on time. He's finishing up a phone call but gestures for me to come in. He ends the call, and we get straight to business.

Hal leans forward and props his elbows on his desk. "Let's start with reviewing your last assignment with WindyCity Robotics and then we'll set objectives for the next one."

I usually work with tech companies like WindyCity Robotics. It's fairly straightforward. I nod. It shouldn't take much time to review.

Hal continues, "How did you get Chad Fitzgerald back? I know you had to play hardball."

I did have to play hardball. That's how I ended up sharing his office chair, leading him to believe we were on the brink of a torrid romance. I leave all that information unsaid. "Not really, recruiting Chad was easy enough."

Hal raises an eyebrow and I know he doesn't believe it was easy. "What did you do, exactly? He was adamant about not returning."

I don't want to share all the details and I keep things vague. "Chad is a nerd. Total geek. I doubt he's ever had a date before. I promised him I'd attend that charity gala as his date if he would sign a contract with a salary increase. I canceled though - left a sweet message with my unfortunate change of work schedule that wouldn't allow me to attend." I hightailed it out of town just 24 hours before the gala. Chad would have held me to my commitment if I was anywhere in town. He's ruthlessly stubborn.

Hal has a sly smile and even laughs. He tends to be grumpy, but he's in a good mood today. It's nice.
"That's why he isn't happy. I'd heard rumblings, but nothing concrete. You know, Viv, that was a risky move."

"Why?" I shrug and then continue. "He had already signed the paperwork." I probably didn't even need to offer the date.

I wore my lucky black skirt, a professional but still short and fitted skirt to my interview with him. I crossed my legs and strategically allowed it to ride up high on my thighs, a trick my stylist taught me when I was first hired at Aberlin. I had the move down to an art. I would've never guessed it would work, but it does with the geeky professionals I usually encounter. Men were so easy to manipulate sometimes.

Hal points his pen at me. "Viv, I know you don't want to hear this… but at some point, you may have to do more than make empty promises. Like actually attending a charity gala."

I feel my shoulders tense a bit and I force myself to relax. "We've covered this topic already, Hal. I don't go there because more is expected than just the date." I know some of the other female consultants will offer up pretty much anything. *I can flirt and tease, but I'm not doing more.*

"I know you're smart and that should be enough to grant you success in this business. It doesn't always work that way. That's just not the world we live in." Hal rests his face on his hand. He looks tired today.

"I know, but that's my boundary." Although to be fair, the boundary blurred a bit with Chad. I feel a pang of guilt that I try to squash down. I expected Chad to play the game, but I didn't expect him to like me and think it was real.

Hal waves a hand dismissively. "Alright, I will give you that it has worked so far, but only time will tell if it will continue to work. I'll drop it. For now."

I decide a subject change is needed. I have information that will make Hal forget about my unwillingness to be a prostitute. I smirk and pause before I continue. "I may have also indicated that I would change Chad's contract to a one-year contract instead of a two-year one, but conveniently forgot to update that little tidbit of information in the final draft." Aberlin gets paid for every one-year contract we secure on the WindyCity assignment, but we get a hefty bonus if employees sign for two years.

"Another risky move, Viv. A smart move. I take it Chad didn't read the contract?"

He didn't. He was too busy looking at my legs to be bothered with the details. "I would have changed it if he had said something - a one-year contract is better than nothing, obviously.

He didn't even glance over the final contract and signed it immediately. Who knows if or when he realizes he signed a two-year contract."

"It's his own fault for not reviewing the paperwork. We can claim it was a simple clerical error if it comes back to bite us. You did good work, Kid. Our client is happy and their workforce has stabilized thanks to your efforts."

Hal pauses and shuffles some paperwork around. "Let's move on to the hospital assignment. This one might be a doozy. For starters, we have zero clearance to offer improved salaries."

"Really? What do they want me to do? Offer pizza parties? I'm not doing that." Hal knows my stance on pizza parties, it matches his own. Managers throw pizza parties for employee appreciation and scratch their heads when they get resignation letters. Seriously pizza parties. It's my number one pet peeve. Nothing says your company is a cheapskate more than a pizza party.

Hal chuckles. "They did mention that, yes. I shut it down."

Of course. "The next obvious question is what can I offer?"

Hal pauses here as if he's mulling things over. He spins his pen in between his fingers. "They just want you to appeal to their heart, their humanity."

My eyes widened. Surely, I did not hear him correctly. "I beg your pardon?"

Hal doesn't say anything, just shrugs.

"Are you serious?" Talk about setting me up for failure. Geez.

"I'm afraid so. Keep in mind that healthcare workers are not like us, they're empaths. It's a weird group of people. They care about others."

"I need to be able to offer *something*, empaths or not." I've been researching healthcare salaries as part of my prep. It's a bit abysmal.

He hands me a folder of paperwork. Try as he may, Hal can't manage to go fully digital. "The first assignment is in Charleston, SC. The hospital there has a ton of open positions. I can't remember exactly how many, but it's plenty. The administration team has cleared you to move people around as you see fit. Especially if it means bringing back someone who has left. But you can move anyone around that you need to. Move people around if it keeps people happy or if it stabilizes the loss of staff. If you can figure out how to use that angle, you can offer more money by moving people to open positions. Assuming those positions pay more, of course."

That would take some creative finagling, but it's something I could do. *I see a fun, color-coded chart in my future!* "Anything else to sweeten the pot?"

"Yeah, one more thing. They have a tiered system of paid time off. You can bump people up to the next tier. Keep in mind that the hospital is so short-staffed that more paid time off isn't a great benefit. The employees can't take it if there's no one to cover their shifts. Some people will be smart enough to see that it's just smoke and mirrors to get them back. You're going to have to find a way to sell it."

I sigh. That's not a lot to work with. "Alright, got it."

Hal continues, "Hospitals hired us to save them so they can save others. Bring back the workers who've left by reminding them of why they started. Their patients need them. It's not going to be easy, but there is a message there that might work."
I frown for a moment. "My assignment is to guilt people into coming back." It's a statement more than a question.

Hal leans back in his desk chair, his brow furrowed. He looks at me for a moment before he says, "Yeah, that's it in a nutshell. Listen, Viv, you're not going to get a warm welcome".

Why would I be expecting a warm welcome? Ha! That would be a first. "I know. I know I'm not; I'm never welcomed with open arms. I can still get the job done. I always do. I don't need someone to roll out the red carpet."

Hal's confidence does not seem to match my own. He looks worried. He continues, "It's gonna be worse this time. I just kind of feel it. Our initial focus is going to be nursing and allied health professionals. Rehab departments and respiratory therapy will fall under that umbrella. Especially nurses though; improving nursing retention and recruitment is the top priority."

I chew on my lip as I do a mental recap. "I will work on a strategy. I can create a message that elicits sympathy and reminds them of their calling. Bring to mind a patient whose life they saved.
Remind them their work makes a difference. Remind them that they can take a bad situation and make it better."

"I think you're on the right track. You're going to have to appeal to their sense of humanity. It's different from anything else you've ever done, or that I've done for that matter. I argued they need to increase salaries for this endeavor to be successful, but they're dead set against it."

I take a deep breath and willfully release the tension in my shoulders. I can do this assignment. I'm up for the challenge. I'm just a few more assignments away from being promoted to Lead Consultant. "Okay, got it. Anything else?" I pull out my notebook and jot a couple of lines down. A plan formulates in my head.

"No, that's it. You need to be in Charleston by Monday morning. That gives you a little time to plan. I'm going to have you check in with me more frequently on this assignment. I want regular updates. I expect we may have to solve problems together."

I nod in agreement.

This assignment is uncharted territory. I leave my meeting and change clothes in my hotel room. The next stop is Central Park for a run. As I navigate the busy city streets the feeling of being overwhelmed begins to fade away. The sights and sounds around me are invigorating. I can't help but smile, I love a new challenge. I start my run through the park, daydreaming of the success I'll find in Charleston. *Maybe even enough for a promotion…*

Charleston

Initiate

CHAPTER

3

It's a dreary day in Charleston. I pause for a moment on the balcony of my extended-stay hotel as I watch the downpour of rain wash over the city streets. I'm dressed in my typical business suit and heels, though I wish I had packed some rain boots. I take one last glance in the mirror before I leave. Oliver was right about southern humidity, my only option was to pull my out-of-control frizzy hair into a low bun. I check the time and head out the door, I am *NEVER* late to a meeting.

I close my eyes, take a deep breath, and listen to the rain just a moment before I get out of my rental car. I'm always nervous during my first meeting with new clients. Often it feels like a me vs them scenario when my goal is to be a team player. I already ordered bagels and coffee; any meeting is better if refreshments are involved.

I enter the conference room, exhibiting more confidence than I feel. Right away, I meet Chloe Morgan.

She introduces herself as the Rehab Director. I don't say hardly anything to her - I don't have a chance. She's a bit aggressive but she knows what she wants.

"You are Ms. Ashmead?" she asks, shaking my hand.

I smile warmly. "Yes, call me Vivian. I'm with Aberlin Consulting."

"I'm glad you're here. We need more rehab staff across the board: physical therapy, occupational therapy, and speech therapy. My current staff is drowning in work. They have burnout. I've had to closely monitor the time spent on lunch breaks and deny time off just to make sure my department's needs are being met. We have patients that depend on us, you know. The administration team has denied my request for travel therapists, saying all their money for travel staff has to go to nursing. Which I do understand, I guess, but it doesn't make my situation any better."

I nod but don't get to say anything. Chloe is on a roll, she continues speaking before I can get a word in.

"To top it all off, we lost Eugene Spinner to a medical chart audit company just a couple of weeks ago. He's the one I want back. He's a physical therapist. People loved Eugene.

He is laid back. He kept the tone of the office light. Plus, he's seriously good at his job. Sharp as a tack and has this way about him that makes people feel at ease. All his patients loved him, and I never once got a complaint. He had a good rapport with nurses and physicians, too. I want him back. I *need* him back to improve department morale. I hear that's what you do. You get people to come back?"

I pull out my notebook and jot down the name Eugene Spinner. "I'm not making promises, I don't know why he left, but I can look into it. My priority is nursing staff, but I will carve out some time and resources for your department, too. I do have a question for you. I was looking at the open job positions in your department. They're either as-needed or full-time. Can you explain that to me?"

"Yeah, we have as-needed positions, known as PRN. People in these positions cover when we need extra staff. No benefits, and no guarantee of hours, but the hourly rate is a bit higher. Some people like it for the flexibility, especially if they don't need a set income or benefits. Full-time positions have benefits and a set salary. It's more stable but less flexible. The hourly pay rate is a bit lower, too."

"Is there any way people in your department can advance their careers?" I ask while jotting a few notes.

Chloe shakes her head. "No. In the rehab world, you're either the worker bee or my job as Director. No in-between. I have nowhere else to advance either. Nursing has a few more options."

No career ladder then, that definitely doesn't help with recruitment efforts. I hand her my card. "Thank you so much for your insight. I'll reach out to Mr. Spinner and see what I can find out."

Chloe thanks me, then goes to grab a bagel. I meet some other people, and most of them are surprisingly enthusiastic about my presence. It's a nice change from my normal assignments.

I'm very much a planner and have, of course, a meeting agenda with set times to keep things on track. This meeting will include all the department heads of the hospital. I'm out of my usual element here. It kind of feels like I'm building an airplane while I'm trying to fly it. I set up the first part of the meeting as a round table discussion. I give everyone two minutes to tell me their biggest concerns and needs.

I jot notes of what I hear as people speak.

- *Staff burnout, low morale*
- *Staff wants more pay, better holiday pay*
- *Better security needed*
- *We need more staff*
- *We don't have the budget to keep hiring travel nurses*

Bringing in more staff will hopefully help with low morale and burnout. I move on to the next topic quickly. I check my watch. I'm two minutes behind on my agenda so I jump into it.

"I'll be working on staff recruitment as one of my primary objectives. I've also been researching hospital security. I heard security concerns from you as well. It's not just an issue at this facility but seems to be an issue across the nation. The question is, 'How do we best address security needs?' My recommendation is for a security audit of the entire facility by an outside company." I hear some agreement and some groans. I hold up my hand to silence the naysayers; I'm not interested in their grumblings. "I've reached out to a couple of security firms already. They're going to give me quotes. I hope to have three to four quotes for you soon. Then you can decide whether or not to proceed."

I wrap up the meeting with just some general housekeeping items and mingle with some of the department heads. They elaborate further on concerns. I get contact information for recently resigned employees and reassure everyone that I can help with the constant loss of personnel. I step outside to call Hal and give him an update.

"Hey, Hal, I just finished my meeting with the hospital administration team. I've started leaving messages for staff who have left so I can get a better sense of what's going on. Key things I keep hearing are the need for security, need for staffing, and burnout. And of course, the staff wants more compensation."

Hal chuckles. "Can't you fix that with a pizza party?"

I start walking down the hallway. I can work the rest of the day from my hotel. "Haha, very funny. I'm getting a few quotes for security audits too."

"Sounds good, Viv. Keep me posted."

Getting people who've left their jobs to talk to me is nearly always a daunting task. I've gotten a few people to agree to talk to me, but none who are interested in returning. Unfortunately, I've had a very ineffective start.

The first nurse I meet insists on more pay. She tells me, "I quit the hospital to help my husband run his business. We have a better shot at financial security that way."

"I can give you more time off? That way you can take time off to help him but continue being a nurse. It's the best of both worlds." From what Hal said she probably won't actually get the time off due to staffing shortages. Maybe she doesn't know that.

She chuckles. "I'm not interested in a few extra days off. You'll have to do better than that."

"Your colleagues need you. They're overwhelmed. Your patients need you too. You have the skills to literally save lives. Can you do that in your husband's business? Your work in the hospital *matters*."

She scoffs and shakes her head. "If what I do matters so much then where is the extra pay? I want more money."

"I can look into moving you into an educational or administrative type role, those usually have a raise."

"Sounds boring. Not interested." Apparently, our interview is done. She just walks away.

I meet with several other nurses: some of them moved away, some of them took other jobs, and no one's interested in coming back. No appeal to the heart is working. It turns out the thinly veiled guilt trip just does not work. I didn't realize how much I relied on my ridiculous flirtations to get my work done until now when it doesn't seem to be an option. I pull out my phone and reluctantly call Hal and give him an update.

"I'm just not sure how to recruit without a salary incentive. Appealing to their humanity doesn't seem to be working." I rub my temples, fighting off a headache.

I can hear Hal shuffling papers in the background. He seems more distracted than usual. "Look, Viv, we need at least some success here or we could lose our other pending healthcare contracts."

I sigh, "Yeah, I know. I need a little bit of time to figure out my best approach."

"Keep me updated, Viv." We hang up and I can feel the tension mounting in my shoulders. I grab my sneakers and go for a run through downtown Charleston. It does wonders for my stress level. I can do this - I just need a little time to figure out how to manage this assignment.

I take a quick shower and feel rejuvenated after the exercise. I'm more hopeful, I just need to figure out my best approach. I check my phone and Ada, a nurse who left the emergency department, responds to my message and agrees to meet me. I grab my work bag and head out the door.

Ada is not a coffee drinker. How does that work? How does she even function? We meet at a smoothie place nearby. She's pretty, every hair in place and make-up applied to perfection. I wonder if she looks like that every day. She tells me to get to the point because she doesn't have much time. I'm not sure how people in Charleston can be so direct, yet so polite at the same time. It's fair to say I'm envious of this skill.

Ada tells me she's a private duty nurse now, she works for a family. The father is nearing death, fighting a battle with cancer that he won't be able to win. He's essentially bedridden. He doesn't need a nurse full-time; the family could easily cover his care with a sitter service. He just needs someone to ensure he is comfortable. However, this family has money to burn and they want the very best care. They approached Ada and she gladly left her gig at the hospital.

"Ada, you're a skilled Emergency Department nurse. That skill set is needed at the hospital and not as a babysitter. I'm here to recruit you back. Your department can't manage without you."

Ada smiles. "That's probably true. I can start an IV on anyone. *ANYONE.* I get called for help all the time. I am a good nurse. I'm a good coworker. I picked up extra shifts and worked holidays since I don't have family nearby. I know they need me. You don't need to convince me of that."

She understands how much she is needed. *That has to be a good sign. Right?*

"Okay. Perfect. Then come back. Come back to where you are wanted and where you are needed. Come back to the frontlines. Come back to sticking people with needles and saving lives."

She pauses for a moment. Then, she shakes her head no. "Sorry, Vivian. No can do. I just want a break. I *need* a break."

Fantastic. "Can you elaborate? What about your job made you need a break?"

She looks out of the window for a moment, I give her time to gather her thoughts. "Girl, so many things. Did you hear about the nurse in Georgia who got thrown across a stretcher by a patient? Broke her shoulder. Security was *in the room.*"

I nod, I did see that story on the news. These events are exactly why I need the administration to agree to a security audit. "Ada, that was absolutely horrific. However, it was an isolated incident."

She pauses again, just for a moment. "You seem like a reasonably smart person. I'm sure you know that while this was an isolated incident, these incidents are becoming more and more frequent. Plus the sexual harassment has gotten out of control."

I shrug, dismissing her statement. "It's just dirty old men, right? Well, probably young men too. Just saying inappropriate things? I'm sure it happens all the time to someone as gorgeous as you. Isn't there a way to use your looks to your advantage? That's what I try to do when dealing with men. It makes my job easier."

She continues, "I imagine it's a little different in my line of work. Sure, I can deal with people saying inappropriate things, though it's annoying. My point is, I shouldn't have to deal with it. But it's more than lewd comments."

"More?" I ask, wondering where this conversation could possibly be going.

Ada looks a bit annoyed, but she continues. "A few weeks ago I was working with a patient who was being admitted to the hospital for low blood pressure. She was sleeping in the bed. Her husband was there, mouthing off inappropriate things to me. I just ignored it, I wasn't in the mood to deal with his nonsense."

I shake my head. "Well, that's understandable, especially with his wife in the room."

She pauses here, taking a sip of her smoothie and gathering her thoughts. "There's more. I was grabbing some extra linen out of the cabinet and he came up behind me, wrapped his arms around me, groping me. I pushed him off easily enough. A male colleague offered to swap patients with me. I saw him lurking around the employee parking lot as my shift ended. I had to run to my car. I was never so happy to leave work.”

My eyes widened, “Why didn’t you call Security? Did you report his behavior?”

Ada looks out the window. “No, it’s not uncommon. We’re basically just told to deal with it and only call Security if things get violent. Of course, it’s too late then. I’ve started taking martial arts. If I ever go back to the hospital again, I need to be able to protect myself.”

“I’m working on getting more security measures implemented,” I add, though I’m beginning to wonder if that’s enough to convince people to come back.

Ada is put together flawlessly, but I can see some of the fatigue in her eyes. “Look, I understand what you’re trying to do. I may return one day, I love the fast-paced emergency department feel. Right now, I need a break. I am taking a break. Could you help me secure a position if it’s months down the road? Maybe I could come back to something better if I had your help.”

Her answer isn’t a no. Not completely. “I don’t know how long my assignment will last here, but I’ll help you if I can. I’d like to get you back sooner, though.”

Ada rests her chin on her hand. "My mental health has suffered the past couple of years. I'm taking a cushy job while it lasts. I'm not coming back, Vivian. Not now anyway."

Ada starts to leave, I stop her by saying, "Ada, just one more question. How on Earth does your hair look so good? This humidity is not working for me…"

Ada laughs. She sends me the link to some kind of hair serum she swears is magic. I sure hope she's right, my hair needs some serious help.

As she leaves I jot a note to follow up with her in a few weeks. The nursing shortage isn't going away overnight.
I wonder if giving staff the option for an extended leave would help with the burnout. Although that wouldn't help with current staffing issues.

I stay at the smoothie place and pull out my laptop to work. I glance at my notes and remember that Chloe, the Rehab Director, asked me to reach out to the physical therapist who left. I Google his name, Eugene Spinner, and don't find much. He doesn't seem to be on any kind of social media. After further research, it looks like he's probably making more money in his new job as a Chart Auditor. *Fantastic.* I send him a text and ask if he'll meet with me. Without the ability to improve his salary, this feels a lot like shooting for the moon.

I spend the next few days interviewing nursing personnel who recently left. I interview exactly fifteen nurses and only one, ONE, agrees to come back if she can switch departments. *That's a disgraceful success rate so far.*

I collapse into my bed exhausted and fighting another headache. I'm really not sure what to do here. These interviews are both futile and draining.

While no one wants to return to work, people in Charleston are a friendly bunch who like to meet and greet. I'll take what I can. Helen returns my call - a nurse who recently resigned agrees to meet with me. She left her job after being a nurse on a surgical unit for at least 20 years. I can't seem to dig up her start date, it was so long ago. I did some social media digging and found out she's in her early 60s and is working stocking shelves at a grocery store now.

Really.

Shelf stocking!? This woman has the ability to save lives, has very likely saved lives, and she's stacking cereal boxes. It's a waste of her skill set. Frankly, it's unacceptable. It's just not how society is supposed to work.

Helen wants to talk. It doesn't take long to realize that she agreed to meet because she loves to talk. She talks to the coffee shop clerk, and the little girl passing by with her mom.

To me. To other random strangers. She has endless words. It takes some effort to focus her on topic.

I jump into the conversation the second I get the chance. "Helen, why did you leave nursing to stock shelves? Help me understand. Why walk away from being a hero?"

She snorts. "Look, as a nurse, on the rare occasion you're the person that saves someone's life, it's special and I remember those moments. I don't take them for granted. But you lose some too. You watch helplessly as the color drains from their face and they leave this world. Neither situation makes me a hero. It simply means I had a job to do, so I did it."

I look at her intently. "You still have a job to do. People need your skills and your abilities. They're not coming home to their families. They're not returning to their lives. Without nurses - nurses like you - these people are *dying*. Filling up the morgues. What you do is crucial to us, all of us. Society needs you in a hospital. Not stocking shelves. Anyone can stock shelves. Not anyone can save lives."

It was a well-rehearsed speech and I delivered it quite flawlessly, if I do say so myself. Only one problem - it was the exact wrong thing to say. I knew that almost immediately as I watched her entire demeanor change.

Helen's jaw clenches and she crosses her arms. "No."

I look at her, clueless. Oh, I am acutely aware of her body language changing, but I don't know why. "I beg your pardon?"

"I said 'No.' I mean it, too. You don't get to do that. Not anyone. Certainly not you, little Miss Fancy Shoes! You don't get to try to make me feel guilty."

I bristle at this statement. Just because I dress nice doesn't mean I don't work hard. I know becoming reactive isn't going to help things, so I shove the emotion down. Everything is so much more casual in Charleston, maybe I should rethink my wardrobe. I'd love to get some new wedge sandals; the heels I'm wearing are killing my feet.

"I gave over 30 years to nursing. I can't tell you how many times someone has vomited on me. Or worse. I always kept clean shoes and scrubs in my locker. I've been groped by more dirty old men than a stripper on half-price beer night. I've been exposed to shingles, scabies, flu, lice, and COVID. And that was just in the last year I worked. I've had needle sticks. I've had blood splatter on me. I've had back injuries from assisting patients. I've been terrified as families screamed in my face."

She pauses here, just a moment to catch her breath. Then she continues, "Do you know what they said to me last time someone screamed in my face and threatened me?"

I just shake my head no, feeling it's important to let her talk.

"Administration said that I needed to work on my customer service skills." She shifts in her seat as if recalling this bit of information makes her uncomfortable.

"Administration said that!?" Whenever I'm on a job, I always say I want to hear the stories of former employees. It's not always true. But I am totally invested in Helen's story. I have a suspicion that the things she tells me will be helpful as I navigate forward.

She appears a little sad. "I was scared. I mean, I was *terrified*. The man screaming at me outweighed me by 100 pounds or more. He had me cornered in a room, in my face. If I knew that was all it was gonna be - just an overgrown kid having a temper tantrum - well, that's one thing. But people are crazy now. I'm strong, but I do not know that I'd be strong enough if he had turned physically violent. The administration team called me in - everyone heard the ruckus. Asked me if there was a way I could have de-escalated the situation."

I look up from the notes I am taking. "Is there a way to de-escalate situations like that?"

Helen shoots me a look.

I hold up my hands defensively. "I'm asking for my own knowledge. No judgment or accusations here."

"Fair enough. Sometimes you can. Sometimes you can't. This time I couldn't. Wanna know the kicker? This guy had caused trouble before, on another unit. It wasn't just me. He wasn't even a patient, just there visiting. I threw my badge on the desk and walked out. I didn't even give notice."

I nod sympathetically. "Did anyone call Security?"

Helen rolls her eyes. "Yes, but we don't have enough security and it takes them time to get there. Violence tends to happen fast and security is just there to clean up the aftermath. I can't do it anymore. I'm done."

"Are you happy? Stocking shelves?" I rest my head on my hand. The weight of it seems heavy. I do think shelf-stocking is a waste of her skills. However, can I really blame her for leaving? This industry is not like the technology industry. People leave tech jobs for better benefits or more money.

Helen left healthcare because she didn't feel safe. Helen's reason for leaving is completely justifiable. *Fantastic.*

She shrugs and plays absently with her empty coffee cup. "I don't know. It's honest work and I got a pay raise after six months. No one has threatened me."

How can I possibly talk her into coming back? I decide to appeal to her ego. "Helen, I've talked with your former coworkers and management. They love you. You're not just a nurse, you are a *good* nurse. You're missed. They want you back. You're not just another colleague. You're a friend. What would it take to change your mind?"

Helen pauses a moment as if considering my question. "I understand what you're trying to do, Vivian. The world needs nurses. The nurses we have are so overworked they can't see straight. It's not going to be easy. Society has never respected nurses. I'm not sure why, maybe because the majority are women. Maybe it's because people are just crazy. But since the pandemic? The treatment of nurses has gotten much worse. Violence against us is rising. There's research out there showing that. I do miss my team. But not enough to go back."

She starts to leave but I stop her as an idea suddenly hits me. I need to do whatever it takes to start making some progress. "Helen, what if I could get you a desk job? Using your skills as a nurse in more of an administrative capacity?"

She's standing next to her chair but I notice a subtle hesitation. "I don't know, Vivian..."

Initially, I thought a liaison to the university needed to be someone young and energetic. I was wrong, it needs to be Helen in that role. *She's a perfect fit.* I play my cards carefully. "I need a liaison to the university. I need someone who knows the ropes. Someone who is not just a nurse, but a *good* nurse."

Helen slowly sits back down. "I'm listening..."

"It would involve recruiting recently graduated nurses to the hospital and placing them in the right departments. I'm looking for someone who can read people, understand their strengths, and place them where they will thrive. I want nurses to be happy. I need them to stay."

Helen looks at me and I meet her gaze. I wonder what she's reading in my eyes. I hope it's not desperation, though desperation is present, no doubt. She finally responds, "I'd be good at that."

I smirk. *I've almost got her.* "I know."

Helen laughs. "Okay, little Miss Fancy Shoes, let me think about it. I swore I would never darken the doors of that place again."

"I'll send you a job description and salary details. It's more money than you were bringing in before. It's definitely more than you make stocking shelves. I want you to have all the information you need to make the right decision." The right decision, of course, is coming back to work for the hospital, so I can finally start showing Hal that I am making progress.

Helen grins. "I might have been wrong about you, I think I like you."

I laugh. "What can I say? I grow on people. You might be right about these shoes though, my feet are killing me."

Helen laughs too. It's nice the mood has lightened. "You look good, girl, but you do need better shoes. Those things will ruin your feet. I'll think things over, stocking shelves isn't easy work either. Easier than being a nurse, but it makes my back sore."

I hand her a business card and she leaves. A sense of relief washes over me. I'm pretty confident Helen will accept the position, even if she left previously for totally justifiable reasons. She's not the type to respond well to me pushing

her for an answer. She just needs a little time to talk herself
into it.

Introduction

I spend the next day at my hotel doing phone interviews. My preference is doing interviews in person, but often people aren't willing to meet and a phone call is the best I can manage. All of them are saying the same thing - too much burnout, too much risk, everything is just too much. *I wonder if this job is too much.* I am just about to think that today has been a total waste when I get a text from the physical therapist who recently left to audit charts.

Eugene Spinner agrees to meet me after work today. It only took me leaving him five messages. He's the first guy I have been able to schedule for an interview, so I put on my lucky black skirt and head to the coffee shop.

Eugene walks in wearing a white button-down shirt with the sleeves rolled up, jeans, and flip-flops. The one picture I could find of him online does not do him justice. At all. He's effortlessly attractive. He's around my age I think - maybe late 20s or early 30s.

I doubt he's even been out of school for a decade. Why would he leave his career as a physical therapist so young? To review medical charts? It's baffling.

We chat about Charleston for a few moments while ordering coffee. Eugene loves Charleston. Hearing him talk about it, you would think it's the best place on Earth. It's easy to see why Chloe wants him back. He's friendly and charming. No doubt his presence would improve staff morale.

We grab our coffee and take the last two seats available on a small couch. We don't have much space between us and I hope I can use the proximity to my advantage. As soon as we're seated I start with my sales pitch. "Eugene, I am here to recruit you back to your former position. Your team was short-staffed before you left and now they're drowning. Absolutely drowning. They don't have someone of your skill set to cover the cardiac unit. It takes a special person to cover cardiac care. You are that person. They haven't been able to fill your shoes." I have no idea if any of that is true, I just know that Eugene routinely covered the cardiac unit and a little flattery never hurts.

He looks bored, which is annoying. This conversation just started. "Are you here to offer me more money? My new position pays me better."

I take a sip of coffee. I've learned to never rush the conversation. "I've looked into it - your current job does pay better, but not much better. I can bump you up to the next tier of time off if you come back."

"Time-off? What good does that do me? We're too short-staffed, I can never take it."

Hal was right, some people see the smoke and mirrors of that offer. I smile and cross my legs, letting my skirt ride up. Eugene notices - I'm sure of it - but it doesn't seem to make a huge impression on him. Guess I'm going to have to go with practicality here. "You're right; it's not a huge benefit if you can never take it. But if I can get your department restaffed, then maybe that could change."

He shrugs. "If you're not here to offer me money, I think our conversation is over."

Over? Ha! *I'm not giving up that easily.* "Maybe it's not about money. It's about your skill set. It's about the patients who need you. You're an integral part of the healthcare team. Your hospital cannot keep losing people."

"If I'm so important, pay me more." He's not angry, not even snarky. He's just matter of fact. He has a point and I'm losing ground.

I need a new tactic, fast. I knew finances would be a hurdle. "Isn't your new job, oh I don't know… atrociously BORING?" I tease, trying to sound somewhat flirtatious. I can't seem to pull it off today.

Regardless of my lack of charm, Eugene laughs. "Yes! Yes, it is! It's really, really boring. I just don't care. I need a decent paycheck. Do you know that I have worked the past five Christmases? Every 4th of July since I graduated. Every time bad weather threatens - I'm at work. The random snowstorm we had a couple of years ago? I was working. I get a small holiday differential but it's not time and a half. No extra pay for inclement weather. Just a pat on the back and someone telling me that I'm a healthcare hero. Being a hero doesn't pay off my student loans."

I know from my research that his student loans may very well be in the six-figure range. His financial concerns are not unfounded. "Don't you rotate holidays? Isn't there a system?"

"Yeah, there is a system. The system breaks down as people keep leaving. People aren't going to stay in that department. It's about more than the money."

I nod for him to continue. I'm happy he's feeding me more information.

He lets out a low whistle. "So many things. Everything is super micromanaged. When I can start my day. When I can end it. When I take lunch or even a break has to be on a specific schedule. The director is more worried I might take an extra five minutes for lunch than actually running a decent department."

Interesting. "Chloe? I met her the other day. She doesn't seem that unreasonable."

"She is absolutely that unreasonable. To be fair, I imagine she gets a good bit of pressure from the higher-ups."

Hmmm… I wonder how much of that is true. "What kind of education do you have? A master's degree?"

"I have a doctorate."

I smirk. "Dr. Spinner…you have a lot of education for someone to be telling you when to take lunch."

Eugene laughs and it makes me laugh, too. "You got that right. But that's how most rehab departments are run. Not just my former department."

Chloe did say she had to run a tight ship to get things done. Most people don't respond well to micromanagement.

I can't help but wonder if Eugene is exaggerating about the extent of it. I'll need to dig into this more.

Without encouragement from me, he continues. "It's all productivity-driven. How much can I bill today? Zero flexibility. I have a list of patients to see, what difference does it make when I see them? I've always gotten my work done."

Fantastic. Sounds like he left for perfectly justifiable reasons too. Maybe he can forget that if I'm a bit more charming. I lean in, just a little. "You want more flexibility? More autonomy?"

"Exactly. My new job doesn't care when I work. As long as I'm doing my assigned tasks no one is breathing down my neck. I don't have to work holidays or weekends. I work from home so inclement weather is not an issue. I just joined a new gym since I can take a break to work out in the middle of the day. I don't care how boring it is - I'm not giving it up."

"I can work with your department to fix these issues. It's part of what I do. I need you to come back, I need your help. I need your influence. Let's fix this, we can do it together. Let's return you to the frontlines where you're so desperately needed. Back to what you were made to do." I know it sounds corny, but I say it anyway. I mean it, too.

"No." Eugene crosses his arms. He has nice arms. *It's distracting.*

"It's where you belong." I smile and lean in just a bit more.

'No."

"It's what you trained to do. For *years…*"

"No." He grins as if he's enjoying our game.

"Listen to reason here. It's where you're most needed."

He shrugs. "The answer is no. Hard pass."

I sigh. Another loss, it stings. *Am I losing my mojo?* "No?"

"No. If I was so desperately needed, I would be paid better. Treated better. I'm treated great at my current job. I make more money, have greater flexibility, and I have the opportunity to advance."

"What if I could finagle more money?" I can't, but he doesn't need to know that.

Eugene raises his eyebrows. "Then I would be quite impressed with your skills."

"My skills are impressive," I say coyly.

He smirks, and leans in; the proximity is unsettling but I hold my ground. He's good, he should be in consulting. *I'd probably agree to a job if he offered it right now.* He pauses a second and then says, "I have no doubt your skills are impressive…"

"So, hypothetically, if I could get you more money…" I lean in just a tad closer. I'm not used to a clientele that flirts back with me. Who knows how to play the game.

Eugene backs away and grins. "I'm always willing to talk money if you can get me more of it."

He gets up to leave and I stand with him. "One last question, Eugene. If you're so adamant about not coming back, why even agree to meet with me?"

He looks at me for a moment. Then he says, "I should apologize. I didn't mean to waste your time. Curiosity, I guess. I've never been a fan of consultants, no offense…"

"None taken." Except yes, offense taken. *Rude.*

"I understand what you're trying to do. Healthcare, not just here but on a national scale, is a mess. Everyone's short-staffed, and wait times to get treatment keep going up. I get it. I even applaud what you're trying to do - something needs to be done."

I put my hand on his arm to stop him from leaving. "You didn't waste my time. The more I can learn about the challenges of working in healthcare, the better. But if you say that something needs to be done, then why not help me, Eugene?"

He shakes his head. "I'm just done with that mess, I'm done."

I hand him my card. "If you change your mind, call me. Consultant or not, I'm good at what I do. I can make your department better. I can make it a place you would want to work."

He winks at me. "That would be nothing short of a miracle. Enjoy your time in Charleston; it's a fun city. Nice to meet you, Vivian."

Eugene waves and walks away.

My interview with him was the most fun interview I've ever had. Something about him not being phased by my ridiculous attempts at flirtation was refreshing. Perhaps

Eugene's not a lost cause, but it would take some serious work to convince him to come back. After all, he said he'd be open to further discussion if I could increase his pay. Not that I can improve his salary unless I find a loophole somewhere. It makes sense he wants more, but that's the one thing I can't give. I'm glad we met, his knowledge gives me an introduction to what the staff is facing.

Pressure

CHAPTER 7

I'm famished and decide to stay at the coffee shop and order a snack. I pull out my phone while I'm eating and see that my sister has called. I feel a twinge of guilt - I said I would call her when I arrived in Charleston, but instead got too wrapped up in my work. I finish my food and return her call.

Lily's cheerful voice answers. "What's up, Sis? Saving the world today?"

"Haha, hardly," I say. "I'm hitting my head against the wall. I've got my work cut out for me. I had a couple of people say yes, one maybe, and the rest have all said no."

She cuts me off. "That's the world we live in, you know how it is. Listen, let's not talk about work. I heard the most distressing news! Oliver is off the market! He's dating a genetics professor. They're pretty serious!"

Distressing news, ha! I roll my eyes. *Here we go again.* "That's hardly distressing news. I already knew about Paige.

He told me at dinner. I've known Oliver for years with no spark of romance. Ever."

"Ugh, I don't see why not. Fine, I guess I can be happy for them. Tell me, have you met a Mr. Charleston, then?"

I groan. Occasionally I will have a short-term fling with someone when traveling, something my sister is way too interested in. I like short-term, how could I have anything more when I am always traveling for work? Besides, I haven't even been here very long. "I'm working too much on this assignment. I don't have time for anything else."

She groans. "Yes, you do. You work too much anyway. Surely you can make time for a Mr. Charleston."

For absolutely no discernable reason at all, my mind goes to Eugene at the mention of Mr. Charleston. "Well, the guy I just interviewed was gorgeous. I wish he was Mr. Charleston. He's a bit out of my league and a work contact - so off limits. But fun to hang out with, even if it was just an interview."

"I seriously doubt he is *out of your league.* You can't eliminate everyone that is a work contact. You only know maybe five people who aren't work contacts, and I'm one of them."

I frown at her statement. I'm happy with my life the way it is, even if it does revolve around work. It offers me stability and purpose. "I don't get involved with work contacts. It's too messy." However, one could argue that Eugene isn't a work contact since he seems to show no interest in returning to the hospital. He would, however, be a distraction. I need to focus all of my energy on this assignment and not on Eugene with his nice arms and stupidly perfect charm. *I'm too close to my promotion for distraction.*

"Ugh, fine. Tell me about work, then." I update her on the people I've met and the challenges I've been facing since I arrived in Charleston.

"You just started, Hon. These things take some time, I imagine."

She's right. *She usually is right.* "How are you doing?"

"Jonathon and I are both working from home now- his office went fully remote. They kept trying some sort of hybrid schedule, but I guess the lease was up on their office space and his company decided not to renew it. I love my husband, but he is around all the time. ALL. THE. TIME. You know me, I need a quiet space to work."

I chuckle. My sister has to totally be in the zone to get any work done at all; she's easily distracted. She used to hide in our backyard shed in high school to do her homework. "You still have the key to my apartment, right? Why don't you make an office there while I'm out of town? I have no idea when I'll be back in Raleigh."

"Ooh… that's a great idea! You don't mind? Can I stock your fridge with fun work snacks I don't have to share with anyone else?"

"I'm paying for it; someone might as well get some use out of it. Though if I come home for a visit the snacks are fair game." I've been wondering lately if I should just cancel my apartment lease and stay in short-term rentals when I'm home. I like having a home base, but financially it does not make much sense. I'm not very attached to my apartment since I'm rarely there. It feels like just another hotel.

"That would be wonderful! I'm sure Jonathon thanks you, too! You may have just saved my marriage."

"Haha, that's what sisters are for, right?"

"Yup! I hate that I didn't get to see you again before you left."

For whatever reason, Lily really does like me around. I tend to take advantage of her generous affection. *I don't mean to, not really.* "I know, this assignment came up kind of quickly. But Charleston isn't far away, maybe I can squeeze in a visit before I go somewhere else."

"I would love that."

I hang up the phone and feel better. My sister is always good at helping me find perspective. Even if she is annoyingly interested in my lack of a love life. Anyway, I'm early into this job, too early to get stressed about things. I'm used to the tech industry, where things tend to move quickly. This assignment is different. I'm going to need an extra dose of patience.

Just as I'm hanging up with Lily, Hal calls. I was kind of hoping the email I sent him earlier would suffice, but I guess not. I fill him in on what I learned from Eugene about the rehab department.

"Viv, you're gonna have to go to that department and see what's really going on. Let's not take the word of a disgruntled employee. Any progress elsewhere?" I agree about visiting the rehab department, though I don't think that Eugene is just a disgruntled employee.

"I think I met the right nurse to work with the school of nursing and recruit graduates. She hasn't accepted the position yet, but I'm confident she will. I just talked to her today, I'm getting some information together for her to review." I may be overplaying my hand a bit. *Saying I'm confident is a bit of a stretch.*

"Do it tonight, we need to get things moving," Hal says gruffly.

I respond in my best fake-smile voice. "Will do. I'll keep you posted."

I head back to my hotel, feeling troubled. I don't know how to make things progress any faster. I uncharacteristically disregard Hal's advice and decide to wait until tomorrow to work on Helen's offer. It's late evening already and I want to think about how to best frame things since this is a critical role.

Instead of working, I take a twilight walk. Charleston is a beautiful city, full of culture and history. I don't always make the time to explore places when I travel for work and I feel a bit of sadness about that tonight. I walk down the street of historical homes called Rainbow Row. The city is busy, but not NYC busy and the sidewalks are easier to navigate.

I find a place to sit overlooking Charleston Bay and try to clear my head. I do some deep breathing as I look over the water, trying to ward off the stress closing in on me. Hal has put a lot of pressure on me by sending me to Charleston. It's Aberlin's first healthcare contract and whether we get more will depend on my results here. *Hal wouldn't put me here if he thought I would fail, right?* Certainly, my paving the way for these new contracts will be enough to land me that promotion.

Progress

CHAPTER

8

As the sun rises the next day, so does my outlook. I completely overslept my alarm but it's still fairly early. I pull together a job description and salary information for Helen. I send her an email about setting up a time to meet. She calls me just a few minutes after I hit send and is happy to meet me before she heads to work today. I quickly dress, skipping the heels this time, and we meet at her favorite coffee shop.

I barely even get into my spiel before she accepts. She's so excited about the nursing liaison position and I don't even have to talk her into it. I wonder why no one thought of placing her in an administrative role before. Instead,
they let a long-term employee just walk away.

"Vivian, you might've been right. Now, don't let that get to your head or anything." She pats my hand and chuckles. "I've been thinking about what you said and I agree stocking shelves was not the best use of my skills."

I haven't even gone over the whole job description with her yet. "Helen, the nursing liaison position involves some teaching and some desk work. Where I really need help is recruiting nursing students to work at the hospital. I need someone helping me fill all these open job postings."

She claps her hands together. "I can do that. I love working with those kids. It makes me feel young! I always unofficially did job counseling for the nursing students anyway."

Her enthusiasm is infectious. I'm genuinely happy for her - this will be a great job for her for the next few years. Hopefully, until she's ready to retire. "I think this is a win for everyone. I'd also like to start some kind of campaign with other nursing schools in the state. I'd like to team up with you and brainstorm some ideas."

Helen holds out her hand. "You got a pen I can borrow?"

I hand her a pen and she starts drawing on the back of the job description. I can't quite make it out until she turns it around. It's a sketch of the ocean sunrise with the words "Work here, live here, play here" on it.

I study the sketch a moment before it sinks in.

I then look up at Helen. "This sketch, you just came up with this? As a marketing idea?"

"Yeah! Charleston is a great place to live. Using that idea would extend our reach beyond local universities and maybe recruit from around the state or even further."

The sketch she's showing me is pretty impressive. "You just came up with this idea, just off the top of your head?"

She looks a little sheepish. "Well, yeah. It's not brilliant, just a thought."

I tap on her sketch with the tip of my pen. "It absolutely is brilliant. This idea is great marketing. I thought you were a good fit for this position, but I was wrong." I shake my head.

She looks up at me.

I continue, "You're a *perfect* fit."

Helen beams. "You think so?"

"I know so."

She creases her brow, looking over the design. "I don't know how to make it into digital ads. I just know how to sketch things out."

I wave my hand dismissively. "You let me worry about the digital piece." Digitizing things is the easy part, I can get that done today.

"I think this job is going to be fun!" Helen's excitement is unmistakable.

I take out my phone to snap a picture of her design. "Welcome back, Helen. Your manager was a fool to ever let you leave."

She hugs me. It's tight and warm - I can barely breathe. It's so sweet and comforting; I'm not complaining. Her excitement is contagious and I can't wait to get her started in her new role.

I email the hospital administration team to expedite Helen into this new position; I don't want anything to slow her down. She said she could start to transition into her role as early as next week. I smile and feel some tension release from my shoulders. It's just one position hired from my list of many, but it's a crucial one. Helen is perfect for it.

I play around with some graphics using her sketch and get something pretty close to what she drew. I send it to her asking her if the color scheme I chose works with her vision.

I'm working on catching up on some other emails when Helen answers back that no one has ever asked about her vision before. She gives me recommendations for some minor tweaks and I send it back. Before long we agree on a design and I order marketing materials to be sent to her new office.

I love setting people up in new positions. I get lost in my work as I make Helen a calendar of when nursing schools around the state graduate. I also include career fairs that I find online. I want Helen to be successful - for her benefit and mine. This work is what I find the most fulfilling. Often when people are new hires, they're overwhelmed and aren't sure where to start. If I can give them a plan to find their footing, that's beneficial for everyone.

I have a pretty solid plan for her to use to get started. I send her my ideas, making sure to indicate it's just a guideline of suggestions. She has the autonomy to change things as she sees fit. That thought makes me wonder how other hospital departments are run. If Chloe had given Eugene some autonomy, would he still be a part of the rehab department?

I decide to investigate that thought and send a text to Eugene:

> Interviewed a nurse who said that no one ever asked her about her vision. I'm guessing it's the same for you?

I shoot Hal an email letting him know about Helen, telling him we already secured new marketing materials, and that I'm heading to the Rehab Department next to interview employees. I'm hopeful he'll see this as progress.

Eugene sends back:

> Yeah, same. I think it's pretty common with any healthcare job.

I'm pleasantly surprised I can get him to chat with me; maybe there's some hope of recruiting him back.

> I'm heading to investigate your former department, to see if I can shake some things up.

He answers immediately:

> If I could be a fly on the wall…
> Let me know how it goes.

72

I can't help but smile. Keeping in touch with Eugene sounds like a great idea, even if he's a little distracting. I pack up my things and head to my car. Today, I feel like I am finally on the road to progress.

Drama

CHAPTER

9

I've procrastinated going to the hospital's Rehab Department all morning but now is the time. I already have clearance from Human Resources and a temporary badge, so I follow the signs and go straight to my destination. The department is a flurry of activity, with people grabbing various pieces of equipment while coming and going. I walk in and find the Rehab Director at her desk. "Hi Chloe, got a second to chat?"

She looks up at me. "Vivian! Did you get Eugene back?"

I enter her office and sit down across from her. "No, but I met with him yesterday. He's pretty adamant about not returning. Says his new job pays better and he has more autonomy."

"I don't care. Autonomy is just a buzzword young folks use these days; no one actually has autonomy. He needs to come back."

I shrug. "I can't force him to come back. I was thinking maybe we could work together. I work with departments to help people become a cohesive team, creating a place where people don't want to leave. A workplace team that becomes their family."

She waves me off dismissively. "I don't care about any of that! I just want Eugene back. He was a hard worker. If he's too hard-headed to come back, can you find me someone else? Someone good."

Choosing my words carefully, I reply, "The priority would be making sure that anyone I recruit would want to stay. My objective for today is to talk with your staff and get a feel for the department."

She shakes her head. "No."

Seriously? I thought Chloe and I would work well together. Guess not. "I'm not asking your permission. I already have clearance from the administration team."

"I said no. My people have work to do. They can meet you after hours. It's the best I can do."

"I heard you say no. It's not your call. I'm doing the interviews now." There's no point in continuing this conversation to nowhere.

Chloe grits her teeth and her face starts turning red. I wonder if I should remind her to breathe. She doesn't say anything else, so I just walk out of her office. Maybe Eugene was right and Chloe is unreasonable. I need to talk to more staff to get a broader picture.

I see an Occupational Therapist in the hallway and I ask to interview her. The OT looks torn and glances toward Chloe's office. I assure her I have the backing of the administration.

My interview with her goes as expected. She doesn't want to tell me much, only saying she already deals with enough on-the-job drama and doesn't want more. I tell her everything Eugene told me. She smiles. She says that Eugene told me everything I need to know. Except that as a woman, she deals with sexual harassment, too.

I was hoping Ada's complaints of crude behavior were relatively isolated. Although Helen mentioned being groped too. I guess this issue is fairly widespread. *Fantastic.* Add that to my list of challenges. "Sexual harassment? By other staff? Or patients?"

"By patients. Some of them can't help it due to brain injuries, strokes, or mental illness. I can excuse that behavior, though it can be difficult and even scary to manage. It's the ones who know better that get me. Many men have a 'healthcare worker, give me a sponge bath' fantasy. I have no retaliation. No support from the administration. It's easy to say it's not a big deal when you're sitting behind a desk."

We chat a bit more about the department concerns Eugene brought up. She tells me she's working on her exit plan too. She continues, "Most of us have an exit plan. I sell tee shirts on Etsy. It's going pretty well. As soon as I pay off some student loan debt, I plan on leaving, too."

Tee shirts!?! "What would it take for you to stay? To live your calling to care for others? What do you need?" I'm concerned she might be right, that all the employees have an exit plan. If that's the case, then the loss of personnel is just beginning.

My fears are confirmed as a Speech Therapist from the department comes dancing down the hall. I'm not exaggerating; she is actually dancing! The girl has some serious moves. The OT I'm interviewing leaves to talk with her colleague. Which is kind of rude, but I'm too curious about what's going on to care.

The Speech Therapist is telling a small group of colleagues that her husband got a raise - a big raise. A raise sufficient for her to leave her job and stay home to care for her young children. Apparently, childcare was eating through the bulk of her salary anyway. Her colleagues hug her and wish her well. They don't even try to get her to stay!

She goes to Chloe's office to give her notice. I stand just outside the door. I peek in as Chloe is muttering and swearing, her behavior starting to escalate as she gets louder. I start videoing on my phone. It's a bit of an ethical gray area, but initially, I just want it so I can review the footage later. I watch (and record) in complete shock. Chloe starts screaming profanities, picks up a stapler on her desk, and hurls it toward the head of the speech therapist.

She leaves Chloe's office, not really all that shaken after being nearly assaulted by a stapler. She makes a phone call to HR, I presume. She's on the phone saying that today is her last day. She continues to say that normally she would give a four-week notice, but her manager threw a stapler at her head and she doesn't feel safe. I admire this woman. Not for leaving her career, but for the calm manner she handles things.

I walk up to her and introduce myself.

She looks at me, "My name is Mary Brooks. They didn't believe me. Said I was being dramatic about the stapler. They're insisting I give a four-week notice."

I am out of line and I know it. But sometimes to achieve progress, you have to work outside the box. "I have a video."

I replay it for her on my phone.

I send the video to the HR Director's email under an anonymous account I use for more covert communications. I need Chloe called out and probably fired - obviously, this sort of behavior cannot be tolerated. If the administration wants to retain its rehab staff, they need to make some serious changes, starting now.

Hastily I gather my things. No need for further interviews. I have all the information I need. "Mary, let's go to HR together. You need to turn in your badge and I need to ruffle some feathers."

She looks at me quizzically. "Isn't your job to make people stay?"

"I'm here to improve things so people want to stay. I imagine there is nothing I can offer to change your mind. But I hope you will work with me, just for the afternoon. We can use this moment to make things better for the colleagues you are leaving behind."

She smiles. "I do love my work family. But I hate my job. I dread getting up in the morning. The stress of it makes me physically ill at times."

We walk into HR and I demand to see the director, James. I met him in my initial meeting with the administrative team. He does his best to try to kick us out, stating we need an appointment. But no one is in the waiting room right now, I know he has time to see us. Or he can make time.

I walk up to him and say, "James, this is Mary Brooks. She's a Speech Therapist in the Rehab Department. She's terminating her employment effective immediately. She will not work out her four-week notice as she was nearly clocked in the head with a stapler. She may consider not filing criminal charges, that's undecided at this point."

James furrows his brow. "I think this can be talked through. She's the only Speech Therapist we have. She needs to work her notice so we can hire another."

Mary interrupts, "The hospital has been short Speech Therapists for months; we used to have three of us. There's been a Speech Therapist opening posted on the job board for over five months. No one is applying because no one wants to work here. It makes no difference if I leave today or in four weeks. There's no one to replace me."

I'm impressed that Mary puts James in his place.

James ignores Mary. He turns to me and says, "You're supposed to be recruiting staff, not ushering them to the exit! Besides, you can't threaten criminal charges - you have no proof."

I tell James to check his email for all the proof he needs. I watch as the color drains out of his face. "Where did you get this?"

I remain noncommittal. "It's my job to know things. I knew you had the video in your email."

James is furious. "If this got out to the media…"

It doesn't take long to ascertain people's priorities. James isn't interested in making the workplace better for the employees here; he's interested in keeping his job easy.
I don't say anything. I just let the silence make him more and more uncomfortable. He visibly starts to squirm. It's fair to say I'm enjoying this moment.

He grits his teeth. "What do you want?"

I start pacing in his office. The space is small, but I think better when I am moving. "James, I want a lot of things. But first of all, I want a *glowing* recommendation for Mary to take with her today to aid in her future career endeavors. She also leaves today. She will not give a notice."

James reluctantly agrees. What other options does he have?

I continue, "I'll be calling a meeting with the entire Administration Team. Mary was nearly assaulted when putting in her notice. Are your other directors acting at this level of unprofessionalism?"

James doesn't answer, he just continues typing a letter of recommendation for Mary.

"I've also learned the nurses don't feel safe from patient and family retaliation and the threat of violence. Do you want to stop losing staff? We need to get things done. We need to do it now." I pause here, waiting for him to make eye contact.

He hands Mary the letter, clenching his jaw and staring me down the whole time. *Does he think he's intimidating? Ha!*

Hardly. Mary's leaving goes directly against my goals, but she's also proof that poor management is leading to personnel loss. I hand Mary my card as she leaves and thank her for helping me stir things up.

I'm feeling hopeful. Sometimes drama is the best catalyst for change. Unfortunately, when I call to update Hal, he doesn't agree. He's too focused on the single employee lost instead of the bigger picture. He does that sometimes, he zeroes in on a minor detail. He insists I send him a detailed report on how I'm going to use this situation to suit our purpose.

Wounded

"Have you ever zipped up a body bag after someone has died?" Lucas unwraps his sandwich and starts eating. He's acting like having a conversation about corpses is totally a normal thing to do.

What an absurd question. That's not a normal human experience. I just shake my head no. I try to put myself in his shoes, to think of what it's like to be an intensive care nurse. I wore my lucky black skirt, but it feels kind of silly.

Lucas was a Charge Nurse on the COVID unit until a few months ago. He's still in healthcare, working at a private practice dermatology clinic. He agreed to meet with me on his lunch break if I treat him to a sandwich from his favorite food truck. I'm happy to oblige. We sit at a picnic table outside to enjoy the fresh air.

With my previous interviews, I came right out of the gate with my recruitment attempts. It's not working, so I switch strategies.

I tell Lucas I'm here to find out why he left hospital work. I am here to listen to his story. I, of course, have ulterior motives. Lucas knows that; he's a smart guy. I'm fortunate that he wants to talk anyway.

His icy blue eyes meet mine. "I know you haven't. I have, though. I've zipped up more body bags since the pandemic began than I have in my previous years of nursing combined. I've sat with more dying patients in the past couple of years than I have in my entire career. Patients whose families were unable to share their last moments. I had patients who have lived too. But I knew they had a long, hard recovery ahead. If they even recovered."

I just nod, encouraging him to continue.

"My last patient was young. Mid-40s. Had a teenage son at home. Admitted with COVID-19 pneumonia. We tried everything we could to keep her off a ventilator. It didn't work. The ventilator didn't work. She passed peacefully, in her sleep. Unable to fight off a disease we were still trying to understand. I called her brother to tell him she passed and listened to him sob. He had to be the one to tell her son that his mom wasn't coming home."

I have the thought that Lucas needs to share this experience, but he should be sharing it with a mental health professional. I don't say anything, what is there to say? I just nod again, encouraging him to continue.

"Every time I zipped up a body bag and called the morgue, it hurt. Physically and emotionally hurt. But that time it hurt more. So much more. She was my age. My colleague came in early to cover the rest of my shift for me. I was a complete mess. I went to the hospital chapel. I didn't find the comfort or peace I was searching for, but I did find quiet. In the stillness of the empty hospital chapel, I was able to listen to my soul. I was broken. I kept seeing the faces of the patients I'd lost since the pandemic began. I don't normally remember patients. We see so many people it just becomes a blur. But I see those faces; they're burned into my memory. Each one of them haunts me still."

I can almost feel his pain radiating off of him, it's nearly palpable. I completely forget my purpose for being there, suddenly consumed with concern for his well-being. He was a dedicated nurse during a worldwide pandemic and he's paying the price for it now.

"Please forgive me for asking, but have you gotten the help that you need? No doubt your mental health has taken a beating. Maybe your physical health, too. How can I help you? Can I track down some resources?"

He finishes a bite of his sandwich. "Pretty sure that's not in your job description. Are you not a recruiter? I know the hospital is struggling. All the hospitals are facing a nursing shortage."

"Recruiting is part of my role, yes. I don't think I can ask you to go back. You need to take care of yourself. You've already done so much."

"You're a terrible recruiter, you know." He smiles at me, but it doesn't mask his sadness. The smile doesn't quite reach his eyes.

"Let me help you." I cannot believe the salary he was making. I make significantly more than he does and for what? Becoming emotionally entangled will not serve me well. Except with Lucas I already am entangled, and I don't know how to dislodge myself from it.

"I'm doing the self-care things - I see a therapist. I exercise and try to get enough sleep. I'm working at a dermatology clinic where no one is dying; they just want Botox injections. It's not that fulfilling. I don't think I'm ready to go back to working in intensive care yet. But maybe one day."

"Take the time you need," I say, ecstatic that Hal isn't around to hear it. I leave my card and tell him to contact me if he ever needs to. He turns to leave and I say, "Lucas, thank you for what you have done. Not many people out there like you."

He pauses for a moment, then says, "I was happy to do it. It was my honor. I can't do it anymore, though. Vivian, I'm done."

"I know. I understand." I watch him walk away. Hal isn't going to be happy at my lack of success, but for the first time maybe ever, I don't care if Hal is happy or not. Pushing Lucas back into a job where he faced trauma is an ethical line I refuse to cross.

I stay at the picnic table for a few moments, trying to gather my thoughts. I feel the chill of the breeze blowing across my skin. I watch the storm clouds roll in and block the sunlight. The darkening weather matches my mood. I need some sort of reset. I remember Eugene talking about going to the gym when we met for coffee. I text him to ask what gym he uses. He sends me the name and tells me he'll be there in an hour.

Perfect. I can use the treadmill to go for a run and maybe mention the Rehab Director position will soon be available. Maybe hanging out with Eugene is the reset I need. I close my eyes and try to erase the sadness I saw in Lucas' eyes.

The pandemic wounded him. I wonder how many others it wounded?

Heartbeat

CHAPTER 11

I pull up to the gym and talk to the manager about a short-term membership. She agrees and hands me the paperwork to sign. I could work out at the hotel, but there's more equipment here and it's by a smoothie place. It also gives me a chance to casually chat with Eugene. Maybe that's the best way to sell him on the Rehab Director position. I still have to get Chloe fired, so I'm getting a bit ahead of myself.

I see Eugene lifting weights with a buddy. It's hard not to stare. He's smiling and laughing with a friend. He's somehow even more attractive in gym clothes than he was when we got coffee. It's more than just that, though. He looks so *relaxed* like he isn't even reviewing his mental to-do list right now. *Do people live that way?! Surely not.* The combination of laid-back and gorgeous is too much for me to deal with at the moment. I shake my head. I don't need these thoughts, he's a potential work contact. I NEED him to be a work contact. *He isn't a contender for Mr. Charleston.*

Odd that I have to continually remind myself that he is off limits.

I head to the treadmill for an easy jog. I force myself to watch the TV intently and not watch Eugene. I'm distracted by the show and I don't see him hop on the treadmill next to me.

"I thought you consulting types just took a big paycheck but were otherwise useless."

I snap my head around to see Eugene grinning at me. My first inclination is to be insulted, *because rude,* but it's hard with his ridiculous expression. "You thought?"

He holds up his hands defensively. "Hey, I can admit when I'm wrong. I talked to Mary. She told me about you storming up to HR to see James…"

I interrupt. "Wait, wait. I wouldn't say I 'stormed.'"

"No, no. I think 'stormed' is the right word. From what Mary tells me you're a force to be reckoned with; I'd hate to get on your bad side." He shudders. "Rumor is Chloe put in her resignation that day."

Is Chloe really leaving? *What an incredible development!* I cross off getting her fired from my mental to-do list. "What? Really? I hadn't heard that yet. But I have a meeting with the hospital administration this afternoon. One of my objectives was to get her fired."

"I guess she saw the writing on the wall. But, yeah there are all kinds of rumors about a pretty brunette in a business suit stirring up trouble." He winks at me and pauses here to catch his breath. "Anyway, I'm really glad you're here. Mary told me how you stood up for her. You went to bat for someone you didn't even know. You're working on getting hospital staff to stay but you helped her walk away with her head held high."

I slow down to a walking speed so I can better focus on the conversation. "I mean, no one deserves to be clocked in the head with a stapler. It was the least I could do."

Eugene thinks for a moment. "I don't think that's right. Not everyone would have come to Mary's defense - most would have walked away. Mary's a friend. She and her husband have me over for dinner sometimes. Great colleague. I appreciate what you did for her. Many of us do. So thank you. I mean it."

"Well, you're welcome. You can pay me back by returning to your department now that your crazy boss is gone." I flash him a smile, trying to muster some level of charm.

He just laughs at me and shakes his head. "I had no idea what you meant when you texted me about a flying stapler. I thought you were just being dramatic, but Mary confirmed everything. How long are you here in Charleston?"

Dramatic?! Hardly. Chloe has some serious anger issues. I don't love that he's changing the subject, but I go with it anyway. "Hard to say. At least another few weeks, I imagine."

He slows his treadmill to a walk and uses a towel to wipe the sweat away. I don't almost trip over my own feet checking him out. That definitely didn't happen. He continues, "A long time to be away from home, isn't it?"

"Not really. My home is Raleigh, NC, which isn't terribly far away. I may drive home for a weekend while I'm here. I travel a lot, more than I'm at home." I slow my treadmill down a bit more. "I met Lucas today, used to work in the Intensive Care Unit."

Eugene glances over at me. "I know him. How is he? Working the COVID unit shook him."

"He's hurting; he went through a lot. You can see it in his eyes. He smiles, but it never quite reaches his eyes. He works for a dermatology place now. I didn't even try to recruit him back."

He glances over at me, raising his eyebrows. "You didn't? Why not? Lucas is a great nurse."

I shrug. "Like I said, he's hurting. He needs time to heal."

"But you are trying to bring back nurses to the hospital, right?"

Yes, desperately trying. "Yeah, it's priority number one. I just started with rehab because it's a small department and it helped me get the lay of the land. Bedside nursing is the most critical need to fill; it's where I'll spend most of my time."

He looks in my direction with a puzzled expression.

I raise my eyebrows, "What?"

He shakes his head. "I don't understand why you didn't try to recruit Lucas back to the hospital if that's your main goal."

"I'm a consultant, *not a monster*. I am not going to push someone back to an environment that was clearly traumatizing," I say rather defensively. It makes exactly zero sense but I will defend Lucas to my dying breath. That is a hill I'll die on. Okay, maybe I'm being slightly dramatic. It was his eyes that got me. Lucas has an incredible shade of icy blue eyes. They were a window into his pain. I try to push that emotion down but it low-key haunts me. I don't usually let work get to me like this job has.

Eugene grumbles. "I didn't call you a monster."

No, but he indicated it. I decide to lean into the drama. I clutch my chest while saying, "I'm not a monster. I have a real, actual heart beating inside of me."

He laughs. "I know you do."

I shoot him my best "don't mess with me" look.

He laughs again. "Vivian, the consultant with a real, actual heartbeat."

I smile. "Don't you forget it!"

He chuckles. "Have you had any luck with getting other nurses back?"

Ugh, I wish. "Not much, unfortunately. I'm having more success working on the longer-term goal of recruiting nurses who have recently graduated. I rehired Helen as the liaison to the university; we're working on recruiting together."

"I know Helen! She'll do great, she's basically everyone's mom. They need nurses at the hospital. Badly. The rehab department can prioritize their caseload to some extent. If they're overwhelmed they pick and choose the most critical need. Nursing can't do that. "

I hadn't considered that the nursing caseload was totally inflexible. As people are sick and injured, beds keep filling up. From what I read, during the height of the pandemic, hospital staff just started filling up hallways when they ran out of rooms. Everyone admitted to the hospital needs a nurse. "You've got a better grasp on the bigger picture that I don't have. Healthcare is different from other industries I've worked with before. Mind if I pick your brain from time to time?"

Eugene considers this for a moment. He says, "I usually do my cardio around 11:00 on weekdays. It breaks up the work day but treadmills are dull. If you keep me company during cardio, we can chat about anything you like."

"Deal," I say. Then, just because I can't help it, I smirk and add, "It breaks up the atrociously boring workday?"

Eugene doesn't answer, He just laughs and waves goodbye.

I walk for a few more minutes. I debate lifting weights but I need to prepare for my meeting. I grab a dark chocolate banana smoothie from next door and head back to my hotel for a quick shower.

I put on a black business suit and purple shirt. I rush out of the hotel since I'm not sure what traffic is like this time of day. It's not too bad, fortunately. I find a parking spot and walk to the hospital conference room.

I say hi to James who just glares at me. Apparently, I'm not forgiven for sending him the video of the assault with a stapler. In my mind, I refer to him as "Crabby James" and it helps me not take his behavior personally. I stifle a giggle. "Crabby James" should be the inspiration for a new office comic strip. I cue up my presentation and mentally prepare for my meeting as people start filing in.

My presentation goes exceptionally well. The hospital administration team (except for Crabby James) is mostly in agreement with my updated plan. I'm relieved to find there is little pushback.

I verify the rehab manager did put in a 30-day notice, which means I have a little time to talk Eugene into the position. I don't see Chloe at the meeting; I'm not surprised she skipped out on it.

They voted to approve the security audit, which is fortunate since I already scheduled the audit for next week. I discussed hiring Helen, who knows everyone and is well-loved. They want Helen to come back to work in any capacity, so that's good. The bedside nursing shortage is still the primary concern, which means I am going to have to beef up my nurse recruitment efforts even more. We work out a few details and I'm finished in a couple of hours.

I eagerly call Hal to share my success, but he's not as enthusiastic. In fact, Grumpy Hal and Crabby James would make an excellent pair right now.

"Viv, you're supposed to be addressing the short-term, not just the long-term. You're being too timid. You've barely recruited anyone back!"

Hal tends to gravitate towards being unreasonable, but I can usually talk him down. I use my calm, most professional tone. "Hal, I'm working on rehiring staff that have left but that takes time. You know it does. It takes building trust and relationships. These people have been burned badly.

You know I can't offer improved salaries, which is a much more efficient approach. Meanwhile, long-term goals - the objectives that will sustain the hospital indefinitely - are going extremely well."

Hal mutters, "What about that PT you talked with - can you get him back?"

"Eugene? Well, maybe. I'm working on it now. I signed up at the gym he goes to so we can work out together."

"That's preposterous!" Hal curses. "How long will that take? We needed him rehired yesterday. Take him to dinner. Wear something low-cut. Show some skin. Do whatever it takes and get some actual work done!"

Hal hangs up and I'm totally annoyed. Of course I've used the "show some skin" approach before, but I don't like being told to do it. Ugh. My lucky black skirt didn't work with Eugene anyway. I'm happy with the progress I've made and try to put that conversation out of my head. Hal will start seeing the results soon and calm down. Hopefully. I need Hal's support if I want to secure a lead consultant position. My heartbeat kicks up a bit from the stress of my conversation with Hal. How can I get him to see reason?

Proposal

CHAPTER

12

I spend the next morning completely focused on my work. I only stop to eat a quick lunch. While I'm eating I grab my phone to double-check my calendar and see I've missed a text. It's from Eugene, a picture of an empty treadmill and a frowning emoji. I laugh at his goofiness. I text him back that I have a proposal for him if he wants to meet and discuss over dinner tonight.

Eugene agrees to dinner and although I could spring for something fancy, he suggests a local BBQ place. I get cleaned up and purposely wear the most non-revealing clothes I can find - a turtleneck, a simple necklace, and a pair of jeans. Which, of course, is kind of stupid since Hal isn't here to see me. Even so, this bit of rebellion empowers me.

The restaurant has a fun easy-going vibe and I immediately love it. I never enjoy stuffy, fancy dining. I have had to endure many fancy work dinners with stuffy people. I appreciate the change in ambiance that tonight brings.

Eugene walks in wearing a plain tee shirt, jeans, and sneakers. *He's off-limits. He's a work contact.* Or will hopefully be a work contact after tonight. We have an easy conversation as I tell him the broad strokes about my meeting and he tells me about his day. I'm not in a hurry to broach him with my offer but finally, he says, "So. Do you have a proposal? Seems rushed after just one dinner, but I'm quite irresistible. Is there a ring involved?"

He's holding up his hand, examining his left ring finger. I just roll my eyes. I briefly wonder what it would be that be that charming. "Eugene. It's a *work* proposal. I'm here to offer you a job."

He waves me off. "This is a nice evening. Why ruin it with work? Do you work all the time?"

He's joking, but like most jokes, there's some truth behind it. I try to ignore his statement. *I know I am a workaholic; that's just how I'm wired.* However, his words sting me a bit and I'm not sure why. Eugene and I have no connection other than work, so what else would he expect anyway? Lily was right, I don't have many connections outside of work. That thought stings too. Too many emotions start running around in my brain and I start feeling defensive. "Of course this is work. It's a *work* dinner."

He says "Fine. *Work* proposal then."

Everything feels wrong and Eugene seems irritated. I need to soften my approach. "This is about work. But I can let it sit until tomorrow if you like."

He gestures for me to continue. "No, no. Go ahead. I already said I wasn't heading back to the hospital though."

I smile slyly. "What if I was able to finagle more money?"

Eugene tilts his head. "Seriously? Can you offer me more money?"

I smirk, starting to feel a bit more like myself. *This is more fun than it should be.* "Yes. I told you my skills are impressive."

Eugene stops eating and meets my gaze. But he doesn't say anything. He just holds eye contact. It's kind of intense.

I clear my throat and continue, "Not only can I get you more money, but also the opportunity to run things the way they should be run. Creating a team that works as a cohesive unit, respected as the professionals they are. A team… led by you?"

"Wait. Are you offering me the Rehab Director position? Chloe's job?" Eugene asks.

"Yes."

He looks at me thoughtfully, taking a bite of food before continuing. "I'm a bit young for that position. Don't have the years of experience Directors typically do."

Don't rush the conversation. I can see he's mulling things over. I take a bite of a french fry before continuing. "Maybe you are a little young, but you're a good fit. I work with managers all the time. The biggest issue I face is that most managers don't see the big picture. Because of the narrow focus, they lack vision. A lack of vision leads to a lack of inspiration. A manager has to see the here and now but they also need to see the future. I've talked with you enough to know you have both. It's a gift, Eugene."

He frowns. "You've been interviewing me?"

"Getting a sense of your strengths, sure. While keeping you company on the treadmill." Eugene is quiet and this statement seems to annoy him.

He looks doubtful. "We've only hung out a couple of times before tonight. How could you possibly know I'd be a good fit?"

"We've spent more time together than a typical interview. Plus, I know when someone is a good manager. I just get a sense about them."

We both take a bite and the silence extends between us. It's not awkward. I wait patiently for him to think things through. He looks at me and says, "I told you I was happy where I am, enjoying my new flexibility."

I shrug. "You did. You also said you would be open to talking if I could increase your salary. The manager position is a good bump in pay. It wouldn't be boring, either."

Eugene relaxes and smiles. "Not atrociously boring?"

I hear Hal's voice in my head, telling me to push him to accept and close the deal.

Instead, I take a more pragmatic approach. "Eugene, the staff respects you. I've talked with several of them. You don't have to win them over; they already love you. You can take some time to consider it." I pull a folder out of my purse and hand it to him. "All the details are in there for you to read over. I've negotiated for them to consider your prior years of loyalty and bring you in under a higher tier of paid time off. I know that's not much of a benefit, but it's something. Salary details are included. Take your time; read it over. I'm happy to answer any questions that arise."

Eugene takes the folder. "You don't want an answer tonight?"

I do, I mean I really, *really* do. But I don't press, which is unusual for me. "No, it's reasonable to give you time to consider your options. You can read the details later and think them over."

He reviews some of the details as we finish eating. I think I've got him - but I'm not sure. My instincts tell me that pushing Eugene will backfire; hopefully, he won't take long to give me an answer. Hal won't be happy I didn't get an answer tonight. Not happy at all.

Eugene and I are leaving the restaurant when he asks, "Do you want to go for a walk?"
The question catches me off guard, but I nod in agreement. Just a few minutes ago he seemed irritated by our conversation. *Now he wants to spend more time with me?* We walk a bit in amiable silence before he starts to speak. "I have thought about management before. It irks me how

things are run - by hospital management, in general. I have ideas. Ideas to make it better, you know?"

I nod. I know he does, I've gotten that sense from him pretty quickly.

"I don't know if it's what I want, though. Can we talk off the record?"

"Sure. Do you just need a sounding board? Someone to bounce ideas off of?" I'm surprised he doesn't have someone in his life to fill this role. Or maybe he does but I'm here now and convenient.

He shrugs. "Yeah, I kind of do."

"Talk to me, then. What's going through your head?" I try to sound encouraging. Knowing what's in Eugene's head is crucial to moving forward. It's more than that, though. I am genuinely curious.

He runs his hands through his hair. "Being transparent here, doing chart audits isn't completely awesome. You weren't wrong to call it boring. I feel a bit lost. I went to school for this - to be a physical therapist. I went to school for years. But it's not what I thought it would be and now I feel let down."

"Do you regret it? Going to school to be a PT?" I smile sympathetically. He went to school for a long time to feel like his job isn't a good fit. That has to be a hard pill to swallow.

"I don't know. I just wish I could be content where I am, ya know? I know I have a good life and even a decent job. I don't know what else I would have gone into. In healthcare, there's so much emphasis on the bottom line. We're working with people, though. These people have lives that are affected by our actions or lack thereof. Healthcare is a business. I get that it has to be. But it needs to be a business with a heart. Or at least a business with a conscience."

"I agree." I pause to look up at him. A business with a heart? What a concept! What if Aberlin Consulting had a heart? *What would that even look like?*

"For example, I had a patient when I worked on the trauma unit just before I left the hospital; he broke both tibias in a car accident."

"Broke what?" I really need to learn some medical terminology.

"His tibias, his shin bones. Both legs… he couldn't walk - he needed a couple of major surgeries. He needed time in a rehab facility. What we do - not just me, the hospital as a whole - directly affects the rest of his life. We gotta give people the best shot we can. That matters. Their life and their recovery actually *matter*... maybe even more than the bottom line."

Beneath the carefree, laid-back attitude Eugene shows to the world, he has a good heart. A heart with much more depth than I realized. I look up at him, searching his dark brown eyes. "That is exactly why we need to find a way to keep the good healthcare professionals working, ones who get the work done but also have a heart."

"I didn't realize I would max out so early, salary-wise. I have student loans and would like to move to a bigger place than my one-bedroom condo. I'm not broke, but I gotta work. I would love to love my work. Like you."

His salary is not awful, but it's not great for a doctorate-level position. He is pretty young to be at the top tier of his salary range. "Yeah? I do love my job. I want you to love your job, too."

"Would I love management?" He looks over at me intently. We stop walking for a moment.

I answer frankly, though Hal would tell me to use rose-colored glasses to paint a picture he can't refuse. "I don't know. I'm certain you're a good fit for the role. I can't promise you would love it. I hope you will, of course. Management can be hard. It's dealing with different employee personalities. It's building morale and trying to be fair. It's connecting with your team and also with other department managers. You have the skills to do it."

Eugene starts walking again. "Thanks, Vivian."

"For?" I start walking too, matching his pace.

"Thank you for being honest. Being a consultant, I expected you to sugarcoat things and tell me being a manager is amazing. I appreciate the honesty."

"You expected me to be a monster?" I ask, teasing. Though there is some hurt behind it. I'm sure others have thought of me as a monster. *Looking at you, Chad Fitzgerald.* Historically, I never really cared. With Eugene, for unidentifiable reasons, I care.

"You have a real, beating heart. I know you're not a monster." He grins and bumps his shoulder into mine.

"I can give you honesty. Consultants aren't monsters. We're not all bad..." He stops walking again and smiles back at me. His smile is not his usual goofy grin. It's a genuine smile that warms places in my heart I didn't even know existed.

I push, but only a little. "I do think you would like it better than your current position. You are much too personable to just be reviewing medical charts all day."

Eugene laughs and shakes his head. "I don't know about that. I'll think about the job. I promise to give you an answer soon. But no more work talk. It's too nice of an evening."

I agree to no more work talk for now. It's odd since 99% of my conversations are work-related. I usually strive to keep my conversation with work contacts just about work, to keep boundaries in place. Eugene is different. He almost feels like a friend. A fun and ridiculously gorgeous friend.
But a friend, still. A very small part of me hopes he doesn't take the job. He wouldn't be off limits then. It's more important I make progress, though. I won't be in Charleston much longer, anyway.

While we make our way back to the parking lot, he tells me about living in Charleston. I tell him about my sister and the little bit I know about living in Raleigh. He has an older sister, too. She lives about an hour away. We laugh about how our sisters like to meddle in our lives. Before long, we've circled back to the restaurant and I'm standing just outside my rental car.

Eugene asks, "Will you be at the gym tomorrow?"

I toss my purse into the driver's seat and turn back to him to answer. He's parked next to me. He's leaning against his car and effortlessly at ease. "I can be. My schedule is flexible for the next few days. I'll meet you around 11:00?"

"Perfect. I'll read over the job info. Regardless of my answer, I do want you to know that I appreciate your vote of confidence. I'm flattered to be asked."

I smile. "Well, it's not just empty flattery. I really do think you'd be a good fit. I wouldn't be asking otherwise. I am under the gun to turn things around."
"I'm sure you are." He hesitates, and then asks, "Are you a hugger?"

Wait. What? "Do *you* like hugs?"

He shrugs. "Yeah, I'm a hugger. It's a Southern thing, maybe. I'm not sure. I don't want to hug you if you aren't a hugger. That's totally creepy."

I laugh and spread my arms out wide. I would definitely *not* classify myself as a hugger but no way I'm saying no to a hug from Eugene. He smiles back and hugs me, tells me goodnight.

I pull out of the parking space and head back to the hotel. When I get back to my room, I throw my purse on the table and pull out my phone. I have missed two calls from Hal. He's demanding to know if I've "sealed the deal."

Hal isn't usually this anxious and it's getting old. The voicemail tells me to call him back unless it's after midnight. I look at the clock. It's 8:56 pm. I don't call him back; I let him think I'm at a long dinner at a fancy place. I'm happy with my progress and genuinely had a good time at dinner with Eugene. I don't need Hal's grumpiness to ruin my mood.

I'm a little bit at a loss for what to do. It's too late to set up further meetings. I check my email and I'm mostly caught up. I scroll through my phone and see that one of the former ICU nurses sent me a text. I had left him a few messages earlier in the week. After nothing but crickets from him, he's agreeing to meet me tomorrow afternoon. I'm delighted with this news of course, but curious as to why he's having a change of heart.

I pull up his profile. His name is Terrance. He was a nurse in the intensive care unit, the same unit as Lucas. *I hope he's not as traumatized as Lucas.* The ICU lost several nurses. I've not been able to get in touch with the others. ICU is a hard department. Not every nurse is willing to work with patients who are critically ill. It's a high-stress environment. If I could bring back even a couple of the ICU nurses it would be beneficial.

It's still before 10 p.m. when I am done. It's early for me to be going to bed. But my belly is full and my ducks are in a row for tomorrow. I slip quietly into the covers and fall into a deep and peaceful sleep. I dream of Eugene accepting my proposal and finding success in Charleston.

Momentum

CHAPTER 13

I wake up before my alarm, open the curtains, and watch the serenity of the sunrise. Hal has already called me a couple of times. I eventually call him back and tell him I expect Eugene to accept the job by this afternoon and that I have more meetings set up with nurses. I have no idea how long it will take Eugene to give me an answer since I didn't give him a timeline. I decide that Hal doesn't need to know that.

Hal gruffly mutters, "It's about time you got something done. I expect a full report on your progress by the end of the day."

Rude. I find my professional voice, once again, to answer. *Stay firm.* "I understand and I'm trying here. Circumstances are more challenging with this healthcare assignment. Couple that with my inability to increase salaries and it's a lot of spinning my wheels. These challenges are not stopping me. I'm making progress."

Hal gives in a little. "I know, I know. I knew this assignment would be hard. But we have to show progress. More progress."

I end the call, irritated. Admittedly, the pace of this assignment is excruciatingly slow. I really just need to buckle down for a few more assignments, until I get promoted, and have some ability to pick and choose my own assignments. I do a little bit more work and realize I'm about to be late meeting Eugene at the gym. He's already on the treadmill when I get there. I hop on the empty treadmill next to him.

"Yes." He's beaming.

"Yes?" I ask. Surely he's not referring to the job! I thought I would have to field more questions and probably even give him more time.

"Yes. Yes, I'll take the management position. I've thought about it and I've always thought I'd like to try management out. This seems like the perfect opportunity to do just that."

"Seriously? You don't want more time to think about it?" I could kiss him right now, I'm so happy! Of course, kissing him right now would involve jumping on his moving treadmill and the logistics are not in my favor. A twinge of regret bubbles to the surface.

Eugene is now officially a work contact and off-limits as fling material. However, Eugene taking the Rehab Director position is exactly the momentum I need. *I can find a fling anytime.*

"No, it feels right. I'm a bit nervous, though. I've not been a manager before. I want to be better than my predecessor."

I give Eugene a reassuring smile. "Well, not throwing office equipment would be a step in the right direction."

He laughs. "Seriously, thinking about being in charge makes me feel overwhelmed. I did call Mary. She's agreed to return for a few hours a day while her kids are in school, just to address the most serious speech therapy needs."

"Mary? The one that was assaulted by a stapler? She's willing to come back?! Wow." I can't believe it. *Eugene is going to be a great Director.*

"I did have to swear an oath to never throw office equipment around for her to agree," he deadpans.

I chuckle, "Mary's a smart cookie. I'm already working on recruiting Speech Therapists, but I will let you handle interviews. You know, you already sound a lot like a good Director."

He slows his treadmill to a walking speed and I match his pace. He shrugs. "I don't want to be terrible."

I almost laugh. Of course, Eugene would not be terrible. But there's a hint of seriousness to his tone. "How about this? I can meet with you weekly at first. Help you problem-solve, and troubleshoot. That sort of thing. I can help with team building and boosting department morale. Then, as you feel comfortable and I move on to my next assignment we can video chat once a month. I'm not going to leave you stranded. I want to set you up for success."

He glances in my direction. "You would do that for me?"

I smile back. Actually, I can't seem to stop smiling. Eugene taking the Rehab Director position is a huge success. If I'm reading things correctly; the rest of the rehab staff will be loyal to Eugene. No more constant personnel loss. No more people planning to leave and sell tee shirts. I say, "Of course. I can write it into the job contract and make it official. I will wrap it up this afternoon and email it to you."

Eugene thanks me again, though it feels as if he's the one doing me a favor. For just a moment, I feel a bit unsettled. Eugene likes the flexibility of his chart auditor job and I am pulling him away from that. I shove that feeling down.

He's getting paid more with his new position and that should make up for any flexibility he loses.

We chat for a few more minutes about details and then walk out to the parking lot together. Eugene gives me a quick hug and thanks me again. As we're leaving, my sister calls.

I answer as I get into my car. "Hey Sis, what's up?"

She sighs dramatically. "Just miss you."

I chuckle. "I miss you, too. I was thinking about coming home this weekend. Are you around?" I should definitely do something to celebrate my successes.

"I am, but I'm itching to get out of town. Mind if I join you in Charleston?"

"I'd love it." Spending some time with Lily sounds like a great way to spend the weekend. She likes to sleep in. I'll be able to get a few hours of work done before she wakes up and we spend the day together.

We make tentative arrangements and I'm on cloud nine. I head to the waterfront deli near my hotel and pull out my laptop. I start working on an updated report for Hal.

While I'm typing, Ada, the nurse I interviewed who recently left the emergency department to be a private duty nurse, calls.

"Vivian, you won't believe it. The patient I was caring for passed away this morning and my services are no longer needed. Turns out I need a job after all."

"Do you want to be back in the emergency department?" I ask. I'm willing to place her anywhere that makes her happy.

"I want to work three 12-hour shifts. Three days on, four off. Anywhere you can make that work?"

I know from my meeting with the administrative team that the intensive care unit can accommodate that schedule and the Nurse Manager prefers it. "Yep, I can make it happen in the ICU."

"I'll take it. I don't want to go back to emergency medicine right now, anyway."

"I'll work up the details and send them your way later today. Thanks, Ada. And welcome back!" I'm sure my face is glowing with happiness. *What a perfect day!*

I'm focused on getting together job offers for both Ada and Eugene when Terrance calls. I quickly check my notes before I answer. He's the former ICU nurse I was supposed to meet tomorrow. He asks if he can meet me today. As luck would have it, he's near my hotel. I meet him in the lobby and bring him a coffee.

Before I can say anything, Terrance is telling me how he's taking off to work on his uncle's fishing boat in Alaska this summer. He had to quit because no one would approve the time off.

I shake my head. Short-sighted management does favors for no industry. "Terrance, I can make sure you have a job when you come back."

"Yep, that's what I want. I just want a change of pace for a few months. I'm happy to come back in mid-September. Lucas is coming to Alaska with me. He said you guys met. He hates dermatology. He might want a job, too."

I'm not sure it's in me to send Lucas back to the place that caused him so much pain. I make a note to check in with him. "I can make that happen for you. I'm not sure Lucas wants it."

Terrance stands up to leave. "Nah, I think Lucas might change his mind. He just needs a change of scenery. Lucas doesn't know how to separate his heart from his work. He's a compassionate, caring, and amazing person. That doesn't work in healthcare. It's better to just be a robot."

I need clarification. "A robot?"

"It hurts to care. It breaks your heart. Thanks for the coffee. I gotta run."

Just like that, he's gone. I call up Crabby James in HR and tell him Terrance and Lucas are returning in September. I don't know if Lucas is or not, but I want to have things set in place in case he does want to come back.

He mutters something under his breath I can't catch. "No. He can't just take four months off."

I roll my eyes. *So crabby.* "James, please be reasonable here. You're not paying him. We're still going to have a nursing shortage in four months. We need him back. He's taking an unpaid sabbatical and he *is* coming back. I'm not asking your permission. End of discussion."

Crabby James is totally unhappy, but everyone else on the administrative team is very pleased. We now have Ada joining the ICU team next week. She didn't have to work out a notice, so she's taking a few days off and then jumping right in. Eugene starts working with me every Friday starting next week, wrapping things up at his other job Monday - Thursday. Helen will soon transition full-time to her role. I also have several offers out to other nurses who left. A couple are coming back to bedside nursing in different departments. A few are taking education and administrative roles within the health system.

I work into the wee hours of the morning making sure I have everything documented and all my ducks in a row. Since I'm not meeting Terrance tomorrow I can sleep in a bit. I don't have any pressing work needs and impulsively decide to take the whole day off. I've achieved the momentum I need.

Balance

CHAPTER

14

I wake up luxuriously late and have a leisurely breakfast. The weather is storming again, so I decide to head to the gym and join Eugene on the treadmill. We pull into the parking lot at the same time and walk in together.

Eugene says, "Hey! I just need a light cardio day today. I hope you're here to keep me company?"

I gesture to the sky. "Yeah, I wanted to go for a run outdoors but the weather is a bit ominous."

He throws his arm around my shoulders and mock lectures me. "Perfect, I'm glad you're here. Okay, rule number one - no work talk. I know that's hard for you, little Miss Workaholic, watch me climb the corporate ladder and amaze everyone. You'll just have to manage to find a way. Rules are rules."

"I have *plenty* of things going on in my life other than work, thank you very much." *Lies, all lies.*

Eugene scoffs. "We'll see about that. I have my doubts."

"For starters, I can talk about how I beat you to the best treadmill and you end up with the one that squeaks." I playfully shove him into the check-in desk and bolt across the gym. I make it to the best treadmill first… but just barely.

Eugene is acting injured from hitting the check-in desk. He dramatically pulls himself onto the treadmill. "For this, Miss Workaholic, you will pay!"

I'm laughing too hard to jog at this point, so I just start the treadmill at a nice walking speed. Eugene starts off on a walk, too. I ask, "Are you having any second thoughts about taking the management position?"

"Nah, getting to meet with you once a week is a nice incentive." He grins broadly.

I smile back but also roll my eyes. "Oh yes, I'm sure that's what sold you."

"Partially, yeah," he replies as if that tidbit of information is obvious.

"Do you flirt with everyone? Or just consultants?"

He winks. "Not everyone. Not even other consultants. Just you."

What nonsense. "You're ridiculous. Besides, we've been meeting more often than that on the treadmill."

He points at me accusingly. "This conversation is almost work talk."

"Fine," I say. Truth be told, I'm having difficulty coming up with a non-work-related topic. "How long have you been at this gym?"

"Not long before I met you. I have a small workout place at my condo, but I found I liked this place better. It has more to offer. I know the owner. She's looking for a Physical Therapist to rent space here; they would like to offer that service on-site."

"I'm sure that would be great for their clients. Have you ever considered something like that?"

Eugene shakes his head disapprovingly. "Miss Workaholic, that's bordering on shop talk again."

I scoff, "You brought it up, not me!" Really I want to punch him in the arm for that comment. I decided against jumping on his treadmill to do just that.

Eugene laughs at my indignation. "I guess that's true. What do you do for fun?"

I think for a moment. I'm not one to have hobbies, but one thing does always bring me happiness. "Thrift store shopping."

"You do not," he accuses.

Why would I lie about that? Once again, I am indignant. "Yes I do, is that so unbelievable?"

"Kind of, yeah. You're fancy. High-class businesswoman and all that." Eugene waves his hands around as if it completely explains what he means.

"There you go bringing up work again..." I tease.

Eugene looks at me intently, "I'm not. It just doesn't fit the mold."

"I'm full of surprises, Eugene Spinner." The statement comes off as much more flirtatious than I intended.

I remind myself he is off-limits again. No dating work contacts. Not ever. It's been my hard and fast rule since I started at Aberlin.

He has a sly grin. "That you are, milady, that you are…"

Wait. What? "Did you just call me 'milady?'"

He grins again. "Yes, it's a Charleston thing."

"I don't think so," I laugh. "British maybe."

"Well, maybe it's a Eugene thing. I can't just call you Vivian or Miss Workaholic all the time. I need options."

"More than two options?" I ask.

"Of course. I feel like that should be obvious."

I laugh again and I decide there is no way I can jog today. I suddenly have this strong urge to prove I am not Miss Workaholic, though I know it's true. In my defense, I say, "For your information my sister Lily is coming up today and tomorrow. I'll be doing sister things, not work things."

"Miss Workaholic, taking time off and thrift store shopping. The world must be coming to an end." He chuckles at his own joke. It's cute.

I laugh but change the subject. "What do you do for fun?"

"I don't know. Not much I guess. I like to play disc golf. Paddleboard. Watch the sunrise on the beach. I read. Work out. Visit my sister. Travel…"

I interrupt here because his list is annoying. *Who has that kind of downtime, anyway?* "No, that doesn't sound like much at all. Do you even have any free time? I mean, you didn't even mention thrift store shopping."

Eugene laughs. "I don't think I've ever been in a thrift store."

I shoot him a look. "How is that even possible?"

He raises his hands defensively. "What? I shop online."

I continue my protest. "But it's so much fun to see what other people have thrown away. You can find great deals on things."

He shakes his head and laughs. Eugene laughs easily. He makes me think that I'm funnier than I actually am. Probably. He finally answers, "If you say so."

"You're totally missing out." I almost offer to take him thrift store shopping, but I haven't quite figured out our relationship yet. I guess we're friends? Instead, I decide it's time for me to leave. I don't know how to navigate things with Eugene. He's off-limits, but I can't seem to keep him in the work-only zone either. It makes me feel unsettled. I continue, "As fun as this has been, I've got to run. I need to shower before Lily gets here. Chat soon, okay?"

Eugene smiles. "Yeah. Chat soon. Enjoy your time off, milady. Seriously, you work hard. You deserve it."

I smile and wave as I leave. I grin all the way out to the car, even though I walked into a torrential downpour of rain. I'm not too proud to admit that Eugene and his antics are a bright spot in my day. I am more the type of person to keep others at arm's length. It's so much easier that way. Anyway, what is with the nicknames? Miss Workaholic, indeed. I'm taking the next two days off - in the middle of an assignment, no less!

Lily gets to Charleston just as I get out of the shower. I have a two-bedroom hotel room- I like the extra space - so she bunks with me for a couple of nights.

"Hey, Sis. I grabbed take-out. The weather is just awful." She shakes out of her raincoat and leaves her umbrella by the door. She then wraps me in the best hug. *Maybe I am a hugger. Interesting.*

I'm grateful for the hug, but even more so for the food. I'm starving. "Thanks for lunch. What do you want to do today?"

Lily sets out the food on the counter of the kitchenette. It smells delicious. "Are you not working? I was going to watch movies and eat all afternoon while you wrapped up work for the week. It's the perfect day for it."

I tell her I'm taking the day off, which of course she acts obnoxiously shocked about. She, just like Eugene, is always accusing me of being a workaholic. I don't want to get out in this messy weather. Watching movies in bed sounds divine. *I can't remember the last time I was lazy.*

"No plans at all this weekend, then? No Mr. Charleston to whisk you around town?" We grab our food and head over to the bed.

I hesitate just briefly and it's my downfall. Lily can spot any sign of weakness a mile away.

Her eyes get big and her smile is wide. "What?!? Tell me everything. Right now. Leave out no details."

I chuckle and shake my head. "No, there's no Mr. Charleston. I think I made a friend, though. It's kind of weird having a friend, especially since he's a work contact."

"Go on…" Lily props her head on her hands and looks at me as if I'm telling the most intriguing story. She needs to expand her horizons.

I just shrug. "Nothing else to say. His name is Eugene. We've worked out a few times together and had dinner one night." Before she can make a big deal about having dinner, I say "A *work* dinner, Sis. Nothing more."

"Oh… Is he the gorgeous interview guy that you wished was Mr. Charleston? That guy?"

"Yeah," I admit. "He's a work contact. I got him a job in management. We're going to be meeting every Friday about team building and staff morale."

Lily makes a big production of rolling her eyes.

"The difference is we chat about other things, too. Not just work stuff. For example, he also has a meddling older sister." I motion to indicate that she is, in fact, the meddling sister. Though, she is my only sister.

"Haha! I love meddling. It's so much fun. It's one of my favorite hobbies. Seriously though, Vivian. I'm worried about you. It's not like you to have a friend." She squeezes my shoulder playfully.

I ignore her sarcasm. "It is weird. But kind of nice. I've enjoyed hanging out with him."

Lily, who was about to start eating her food, stops abruptly, just before she is about to take a bite. "WAIT. Do you like him, like him?"

It's my turn to roll my eyes. "Are you in third grade?"

She points her fork at me. "Do you? Don't avoid the question."

I shake my head. "He's a friend."

"Friend with benefits?" She grins, staring me down so she can get an honest answer. She knows I can't lie to her if I'm making eye contact. She can read me too well. It's annoying.

"No, just a friend. I'm trying something new. Besides, it's kind of hard not to be friends with Eugene. He insists on talking about things other than work. He's charming and goofy. He can't hold a serious conversation for long." *Friends with benefits, I wish. I bet those benefits would be amazing.* I take a deep breath and clear my head. I absolutely can't entertain those kinds of thoughts.

She looks at me intently. "Interesting. Why the change?"

I tell her something about being in Charleston has me off my game. I get adequate sleep. I'm eating fairly well and working out. I'm making connections deeper than just work acquaintances. The whole thing feels odd. "I don't like it. My job is much harder when I care about the people I am working with. I prefer a cold distance instead."

She reaches for my hand and squeezes it affectionately. "You sound like a healthy, functioning adult. You look good, too. You look great. Charleston is good for you. Maybe you can drag this trip out some. It's nice to see you happy."

This whole conversation is bizarre and I don't like that my sister can see deeper than others and read me so well. I didn't know that I normally seemed unhappy. *I do seem to have a better life balance here.* It's too much soul-searching for me to delve into right now, so instead I grab the remote and find a movie neither of us has seen. We watch the movie, well part of it. We both fall asleep and wake up during the ending credits.

Saturday is much of the same, though we do walk around Downtown for a bit when the rain gives us a reprieve. Sunday is beautiful, not a cloud in the sky. But Lily has to get back home and she leaves early in the morning. I hug her goodbye and check my email. It's odd, nothing much in it. Only a quick note from Hal telling me he was pleased with my report and that he'd check in next week.

Nothing. I have nothing to do. I don't do well with nothing to do, so I write out my plan for next week. That doesn't take long. I straighten up my hotel room, but it doesn't take long, either.

I decide I need some fresh air and I'm sitting on my balcony when I hear my phone chime with a text from Eugene:

How is the visit with your sister?
Is Miss Workaholic taking off Sunday, too?

What is this obsession he and Lily have with my work schedule?! I try my very best to think of a snarky response, but I've got nothing. I tell him I'm off today and that Lily has already left.

> Want to join me at Fort Sumter? It's a total tourist of Charleston thing to do.

Not much of a tourist, but I am already stir-crazy. If I'm honest with myself, I'm a little nervous about hanging out with Eugene. I don't know why. I was never nervous to hang out with Todd - my last fling in San Diego. It's different. I remind myself he is a work contact (again) and text him back to confirm plans. I change out of my pajamas into shorts and a tee shirt. I grab my sneakers and am ready to go pretty quickly.

He picks me up at my hotel, wearing shorts and a tee shirt. I'm happy I got the tourist dress code right, I wasn't sure. Eugene drives us to the Visitor Center. It's a 30-minute boat ride to Fort Sumter, and I learn it played a key role in the Civil War. I find the history interesting, but nothing can compare to the peace I feel on the water. The gentle rock of the boat, the sun reflecting off the bay. I had forgotten how much I love being on the water; I never get a chance to enjoy it.

"Thank you, Eugene. You saved me from an uneventful afternoon in my hotel room and gave me this." I gesture widely at the ocean as if that totally explains how I am feeling.

Naturally, he's confused. "I gave you salt water?"

I sigh happily. "Exactly."

We chat about Charleston's history and the other tourists we see. The conversation is easy and light - Eugene makes me laugh with his very terrible impression of a boat captain. For a while, it feels like I'm actually a tourist on vacation. The constant tension in my shoulders eases. Is this what relaxing feels like?!

We spend the better part of the afternoon at Fort Sumter. Eugene continues his ridiculous acting as the worst boat captain ever. The charade makes even less sense now with a fort as the backdrop and not a boat. I'm trying not to laugh and encourage his absurd behavior, but he soon has me in stitches. An elderly lady stops us and insists on taking our picture because we make the "cutest couple." I'm about to tell her we're just work friends when Eugene hands her his phone and interrupts. "Captain Spinner never forgoes the opportunity for a photo with a fair maiden."

The last boat back is leaving soon, but I've learned Eugene needs to eat every two hours and he heads into the gift shop for a snack. I wait outside and check my messages. I have a couple of voicemails from Hal:

> *Hi Viv, I really wish you were better about answering your phone. Change of plans. Time is of the essence here.*

Next message:

> *Viv!! Call me now.*

I listen to the next message:

> *Viv, I had my assistant set you up on the red eye out of Charleston. We need you in New Orleans for an 8 a.m. meeting tomorrow with your next assignment. The Lake Pontchartrain Hospital in New Orleans hired us with an immediate start date. You'll have to finish things up in Charleston remotely. Your plane leaves at 10:35 p.m. Let me know if you got this.*

I'm concentrating on Hal's message and don't see Eugene come up. "Bad news?"

I look up at him. For someone who's such a goofball, making eye contact with Eugene feels like someone looking into the depths of my soul. Unexpectedly, I'm flooded with the thought that I wish my life was different. That I could have friends and downtime on the weekends. I wish I had some control of my schedule. I wish I could stay here, in Charleston. I check the time. It's already after 5 p.m.; I'll have to leave soon. "I just need to call my boss Hal quickly before we get on the boat."

He nods as I make the call. I hold the phone away from my ear. Hal is shouting, "VIV!!! IT'S ABOUT TIME."

"Hal, it's only been a couple of hours. I got your message; I have plenty of time to get to the airport." Eugene is frowning at me, but I ignore it. Hal's telling me about how word got out that I did well in Charleston; it's time for me to move on. All of it seems quite odd, it was just a few days ago Hal was demanding more progress.

"Hal. I still have a ton of work left in Charleston. It's not feasible to do it remotely while taking on a whole new assignment. We never overlap assignments. It's in the contract for me to train Helen and Eugene." This sudden change in plans has my head spinning.

"Why? Are they stupid?" I give Eugene an apologetic shrug, I'm sure he can hear everything. It's hard not to, Hal is so worked up. Hal continues, "How did you finally get Eugene on board anyway? You never told me. Give him a tour of your hotel bed?"

My face is at least one million shades of red - I'm not sure if it's anger or embarrassment. Probably both.

I cover my face with my hand while answering Hal. What I want to do is to crawl into a hole and hide. "We have talked and talked about this Hal. Many times. You know my boundaries. I'm a professional and not an escort. He came back because I gave him a good offer. I happen to be really good at my job - that's why you hired me."

"Look Kid, you keep telling yourself that. Deep down you know that's not the world we live in. Just get on the plane and do as you're told. It's not a request." Hal hangs up and I stare at my phone, dumbfounded.

I'm shaking, I'm so furious. I glance at Eugene briefly. I'm too ashamed to hold his gaze.

I'm at a total loss of what to do, but Eugene takes my hand and leads me back to the boat. I'm grateful for his guidance as I try to process what just happened. We're on the last boat leaving and it is crowded. I find myself shoved next to Eugene and his proximity does nothing to help me clear my head. So much for being a relaxed tourist today.

After a few moments on the water, Eugene breaks the rather tense silence. "Vivian."

"I would never… not ever …I can't…I mean, I'm…." Words seem hard right now. I'm trying to gauge why I'm so upset. Hal and I have had these conversations before. A voice in my head whispers… *you're not upset by Hal's words. You're upset Eugene heard them.* The accuracy of the thought resonates deeply and I can't fully shut it out. Believe me, I try.

Eugene just looks at me and cocks his head to the side. "Never what? Manipulate me into a job? Give me a tour of your hotel bed? Is that how he put it? Who even says that?!"

I'm sure I'm beet red. "It's just, I mean… ugh!!" Words are not hard right now. They're impossible. I can't shake the thought that Eugene must be thinking I'm horrible and that my success comes at any cost.

Isn't that true? Wouldn't I eventually resort to whatever it takes to climb the next step of the corporate ladder? Isn't that what Hal has not so subtly been saying?

"Don't get me wrong, a tour of your hotel bed's a tempting offer." He bumps his shoulder into mine and grins. "You seem like a classy lady, though. It doesn't seem like that would be your style."

I take a deep breath, trying to calm my nerves. Somehow I've regained the ability to speak again. I don't look at Eugene, but instead focus on the water around me. It has a calming effect. "No, that's not my style. My company does have consultants who will do whatever they feel is necessary to get the job done. Hal knows my boundaries, the lines I'm not willing to cross. We've always had a professional relationship and some level of mutual respect. Although he has alluded to the fact that advancing in my career may require more flexible boundaries, he never pushed me to cross those lines until I came to Charleston."

"But he has done it on this trip? Before today?" I can feel Eugene looking at me. But I keep my gaze out over the water. It calms me.

I hedge, I don't want to have this conversation. It's not fair to avoid it either, so I continue, "Not exactly. He told me to wine and dine you, show some skin. Do whatever it takes to get you hired. He was stressed, he wanted me to get back to recruiting nurses ASAP. I know how that sounds. I get it. But, Hal's been a mentor to me. He's helped me be successful. We don't always agree, but he does try to help me."

"Wait. You were wearing a turtleneck and jeans when we went out to dinner."

It's odd that he remembers what I was wearing. I finally turn towards him and give him a sly smile. "I went a bit rogue. No one tells me when to show skin or not."

"Classy lady, I know. I like that about you. But not as much as I like your willingness to go rogue." He grins briefly but then has a look I can't quite read. Concern? Hurt? I don't know. He continues, "Was any of this real? Or are you just manipulating me to meet your goals?"

It's a very direct question, but it's a fair one. It hurts, even so. I look out over the water again to gather my thoughts. I decide honesty is my only option here. "It's true I wanted you in the director position. It's also true I thought you were a good fit. Hal pushed me hard to get an answer from you at dinner. Really hard."

I can see him looking at me out of the corner of my eye. I keep my focus on the water and try to find tranquility. "But you gave me plenty of time. You weren't pushy at all. In fact, I was surprised you weren't pushy. You weren't pushy with Lucas or Mary either. You talked them out of coming back if anything."

"I know. Typically I would push for an answer, but I didn't with you - I just couldn't do it. I knew Hal would be mad and I'd take some heat for it. I planned on giving you a few days, regardless of Hal's reaction. I wanted to be fair to you. Somewhere along the way you and I became friends. Or I thought we did. I hope we did. I don't usually make friends, I'm not good at friendships. It's hard when I'm always traveling." Apparently, we have arrived at the part of the conversation where I start to ramble incoherently. *That's not at all awkward.*

Eugene doesn't seem to mind my rambling. He pulls me into a hug. I wrap my arms around his waist and lay my head on his chest. It feels good to be in his arms. I get a sense that some of his hurt is still there. Or maybe he's trying to decide if he can trust me. I don't blame him. I do use a bit of manipulation to get things done, I always have. Or at least I used to before Charleston. Interesting that I didn't need to use manipulation for this assignment, yet it was somewhat successful. Maybe I never needed it.

He sighs and pulls back so he can look me in the eyes. "Of course we're friends. I don't pull out my Captain Spinner persona for just anyone." He pauses for a moment before he continues. "Vivian, what would have happened if I didn't say yes to the director position? Would you have tried to seduce me? See if that worked?"

"No."

Eugene shoots me a look like he doesn't fully believe me. Which is fair. I guess. I all but seduced Chad.

My words become more emphatic. "No. I don't do that. I don't cross that line. I don't trade sex for favors."

"But to advance in your career, you might have to?" He looks at me sympathetically. Not a hint of judgment in his eyes.

"Other successful consultants have, sure. They also feed people alcohol or even drugs to get them to sign on for something. That's the rumor anyway. Obviously, it's all done under the table."

"Have you?" His arm is still draped loosely around me, rubbing my back.

"No. Admittedly my company is shady in some of their practices. But you don't have to be - data and numbers are powerful. Working with people to get them what they want in a job doesn't require being sketchy. I'm not innocent, by any means. I've been purposely misleading. Often I'm strategic about what I'm wearing and flirt with men as a method of persuasion. It never goes beyond that. It doesn't always work. It didn't work with you."

Eugene considers this for a moment. "So the clothes you wore when we first met, was that strategic?"

No point in denying it, I'm in this deep. "Yeah. It was. My lucky black skirt."

Eugene smirks. "That works? Don't get me wrong here, you are absolutely stunning, milady. I noticed that when we first met - I'd have to be dead not to. However, I wouldn't take a job just because a hot woman with amazing legs asked me to. I can't imagine anyone would."

I feel my cheeks start to blush, so I look back out over the water. "You'd be surprised. It works really well in the tech industry. I know how it sounds. Hal has told me that my brain should be enough, but that the world doesn't work that way."

His response is nonchalant. "Hey, no judgment from me. I know women have it harder in corporate America. I'm not going to pretend to know what it's like."

"Regardless of my approach, I do try to get people decent career placement. Better than they had before."

"I believe you do. I have a better position. I do have to say that part of the reason I took the rehab director job is because you'd be there to help me. A big part. I'm not sure I can do this without you."

I look up at him and smile. He will do a great job in his new role. "You don't really need me, Eugene."

He starts to protest, but I continue. "I won't leave you stranded. We can still video chat. I'm not backing out on you. And not because it's a contractual obligation. I'll help you because I want you to be successful."

"You want me to be successful because we are friends? Or because it benefits your work goals?"

I shrug and give a candid answer. "Both things can be true."

I think for a moment and feel like I need to clarify further. "Eugene, normally I don't hang out socially with someone after they commit to a new position. I've typically moved on to recruiting the next person. I'm not one to spend non-work time with a work contact. Today is unusual for me."

Eugene gives me a flirtatious grin. "You enjoy spending non-work-related time with me, milady?"

His expression is too smug for my liking. I roll my eyes at him but stick to the truth. "I'm here, aren't I?"

The wind has picked up and Eugene tucks a strand of my hair behind my ear, his tone serious again. "Vivian, I don't like how your boss treats you."

"He's not usually like this," I say, just barely above a whisper. The space between us has diminished and I'm fighting between wanting to wrap my arms around him and wanting to run far, far away where things are simple. *Nothing about Eugene is simple.*

"I should hope not. I'm not sure if you need to hear this or not, but you're more than a pretty face to close a deal. So much more." He runs his thumb along my jawline while he says it, and my entire body is ridiculously responsive to his touch. I contemplate jumping into the ocean just to cool off.

I pull away a little, the intensity more than I can handle. I already have no idea how I can walk away from Eugene and leave Charleston. Every cell in my being is protesting. Loudly. "Thank you, that's very sweet of you to say. I'll have a very serious talk with Hal when I'm not so angry and can get my thoughts in order. I'm so sorry you overheard that conversation. I really am."

Eugene shrugs. "No need to apologize. So you're leaving me tonight?"

I don't want to go. I've never, *not ever* wanted to stay somewhere longer than my assignment. No part of me is ready to leave Charleston. But I will, work comes first. It's always come first. At least until my next promotion. I look out over the water again. "Yeah. In just a couple hours."

We watch the boat pull into the dock in silence. Some of the tension between us has dissipated but not all of it. I swallow the lump in my throat as I think of saying goodbye to Charleston. Goodbye to Eugene. Everything about leaving feels so very wrong.

Eugene drives us back to my hotel. He gets out of the car and walks with me to my room. He takes my hand, his fingers intertwined with mine. He squeezes my hand and grins. "Just trying to keep you close a few minutes longer, milady."

We reach my room and he offers to help me pack or even take me to the airport. It's a kind offer, but I need some time alone to wrap my head around the events of the day. Eugene seems to understand I need time to process so he doesn't argue. Instead, he puts his hands on my shoulders and looks into my eyes like he's searching for something. I'm not sure what he is looking for, but I get the sense he doesn't find it. He pulls me into his arms and hugs me goodbye.

He holds me close and stays there. Neither of us says anything. In the deep and buried recesses of my heart, I know I want to stay. I want to stay here, in Charleston, with Eugene. Maybe forever. I'm not a fool though.

I know that my life doesn't accommodate romance. I know my current schedule will never allow for more, or if Eugene would even want more. Arguably, he's showing interest now, but he wouldn't want a partner who is gone more often than not - who would? Especially not Eugene, who could easily find someone who could offer him more. I just don't have more to give, I belong to my career. He pulls away, perhaps reluctantly. As he does his lips brush my ear and he whispers "I'm going to miss you, Vivian Ashmead." A shiver runs down my spine, but I ignore the sensation. Or I try to, anyway. Though my mind says I can't have more with Eugene, my traitorous body has other ideas.

I'm still tangled in his arms when he pauses and leans forward. It's that exact moment I decide to say the single, most stupid statement I have ever uttered. The words that I would replay and regret in the weeks to come. "Eugene. I have to go."

He gives me a curt nod and leaves.

I want to say something that's not stupid. I want to stop him from leaving but my words fail me again. I look out the hotel window overlooking the parking lot. Eugene looks up and I awkwardly wave goodbye.

A sense of sadness threatens to overwhelm me, but I have a lot of things to do and not much time. I push down all the feelings and start packing my things.

My mad dash to pack and get to the airport is for naught; my flight is delayed two hours. I read through the initial information about my assignment in New Orleans, but it doesn't take long. Normally I do my own research, but my meeting is in just a few hours. I pause my work and text my sister to let her know I'm heading to New Orleans.

She immediately calls. I'm surprised she's awake, it's nearly midnight.

"Sis. You can't be leaving Charleston! It was so good for you!. You were happy and healthy. What about Mr. Charleston?"

I let out a long breath. "I spent the day with Eugene at Fort Sumter."

"I forgot Mr. Charleston has a real name! Spent the day with him, eh? After shirking your work responsibilities with me the day before. That's very interesting…"

I tell her all about my day. She laughs at Eugene's antics and insists she needs to meet him. I am positively mortified, but I tell her about my conversation with Hal and Eugene hearing most of it. If I'm angry at Hal, then Lily is absolutely outraged. Her outrage causes my eyes to burn with tears. She's always had my back, but she doesn't know the lengths I'm willing to take to close a deal. Maybe I don't offer a tour of my hotel bed, but the reality is I'm not that far away from it if I stop to think about it. I'm not sure I'm happy with who I've become. For the second time today, shame nearly overcomes me.

"Vivian, listen to me, dear. You know I love you, okay? But I need you to hear me right now. You don't have to do this to yourself. You don't have to work for your asinine boss. You don't have to take the sexual harassment. You don't have to work absurdly long hours. You can walk away and take your life back. Call him and put in your notice, effective immediately. Come live with us until you get on your feet. I got you."

"I know you do..." I now have unshed tears burning my eyes. I'm unable to shove down the emotions right now. "I can't do it. I can't walk away. I just need to put in a little more work so I can be promoted. Besides, I don't have anything else."

"You have me. You always have me. You can start over."

I swallow hard. My voice is strained with emotion. "It's not that easy."

"No. But it's that simple. Change your flight, Vivian. Please. Come home."

"No. No… I'll establish better boundaries with Hal. I want to take on this new assignment. I can do this. I'm so close to getting promoted."

I hear Lily sigh, I know she's frustrated with me. She's always thought that my career took too much. This conversation just adds fuel to that fire. "I know you can. Should you?"

I hear boarding for my flight starting. "That's my flight, Sis. I gotta go. I love you."

I grab my seat on the plane, grateful that no one is next to me. I go to turn off my phone and see that Eugene has sent me the picture of us from earlier today. I look different in the picture. Happy.

I start to text him back, but the words I find are the words I would never have the courage to say. I turn off my phone and close my eyes. I tune in to the hum of the engine and try to clear my head.

I don't need to leave with regrets; my next challenge lies ahead. It's time for my path to diverge to a new challenge and away from Charleston.

New Orleans

It's absurdly early morning when I land in New Orleans. I'm so tired I can barely function. I tried to cat-nap on the plane, but my stupid brain kept overthinking everything about my day with Eugene. The brief rest I did find hardly makes up for missing an entire night's sleep. I immediately grab a coffee and then go rent a car. I drive to my hotel to see if they'll let me check in early. I'm grateful they have a room ready. I grab a muffin from the breakfast area and hastily eat it on the way to my room. I shower, put on enough makeup to hide the dark circles under my eyes, and then head out for my meeting.

Initially, the meeting is chaotic, completely lacking organization from the administration team. From the get-go I'm irritated. Maybe I'm not supposed to, but I hijack the meeting. I tell them what I've learned about the staff concerns and challenges in Charleston. I let them know I was able to bring back some staff by granting them their scheduling preferences and a couple of promotions.

Many of the employees were relieved safety measures were being implemented. That relief helps retain current employees, which is the most efficient and effective course of action. I tell them I'm scheduling a security audit immediately like I did for the hospital in Charleston. I don't ask for approval. I'm weary and just want to get things done.

I stand up and start walking around the room. Partly because if I sit any longer, I'm going to fall asleep. "The thing is, the hospital staff isn't always treated well by the patients they're so dedicated to serving. Which is an unfortunate glimpse into what our society has become. But that is also a problem we can't fix. What we can fix is how staff are treated by their management. I'm here to tell you - your healthcare providers are gold. They need to be treated like that. Do you want your staff to stay? Then treat them like they're irreplaceable. Because that's not far from the truth. At all."

Henrietta, a Nurse Manager starts clapping, and the rest of the group looks at her like she's crazy. She doesn't seem to care and I admire that level of confidence. She comes over and puts her arm around me. It's a little awkward because I don't expect it and I don't know her. But I don't fight it. I'm always happy to have an ally.

Everyone else is staring at us and she says, "Look, this gal's saying what I've been saying for months. We can't bring in enough new nurses, even with the best recruiting strategies. We gotta treat the ones we got right. We can't keep losing staff."

After that, the meeting adjourns and Henrietta asks me if I could have lunch with her in an hour, in the hospital's cafeteria. I desperately want to go to bed, but I'm also hungry. She did stand with me and I'll definitely need her support moving forward. I tell her I'll head down there and work a bit until she can join me. Her face lights up and she thanks me. It's not hard to make this woman happy.

I have a million things to do to start this project off, my brain is hazy, and I'm having trouble getting motivated. I pull out my phone to check my messages. Hal's emailed me a couple of times, mostly with assignment goals. I see a longer one from him that piques my interest.

I pull out my laptop so it's easier to read. His email is almost an apology. Not quite. I guess he knows he pushed me a bit too far during our last conversation. *He's trying to do damage control.* Mostly he's saying that he is under a lot of stress to move these healthcare contracts forward.
He tells me he's giving me a bonus since I have to wrap things up in Charleston remotely. He's also giving me more money for my daily expenses while I am in New Orleans.

It's not enough. I write him back and tell him I won't be treated like that again, and that I expect to be treated like the professional that I am. He replies immediately with a single word: understood.

I've done almost nothing and I see Henrietta coming to meet me. I close my laptop, so much for being productive. Henrietta and I grab a quick lunch and she wastes no time getting started.

As we sit down at our table she says, "Vivian Ashmead, you're my kinda people. I like you already."

I smile. She's fun, she's blunt, and if I'm reading the room right, she's a thorn in the side of the rest of the administration team. "I like you, too. You really helped me during the meeting. I was flying all night, and haven't slept except for dozing on the airplane a bit. I left Charleston in a bit of a rush."

She's busy eating a prepackaged salad but looks up at me and smiles sympathetically. "Did you want to leave? I love Charleston. I went to high school there."
That's a loaded question, though she of course doesn't know it. I answer truthfully. "No, I wasn't ready to leave. But duty calls and that's why I'm here. After I get adequate sleep and my brain is a fully functioning member of my body, I'm

going to be your biggest advocate. We need to stabilize the loss of employees from here. It's something we can do, but I do need your help."

"Yeah, anything, Love. I'm on your side. The rest of the administration team is a bunch of old dudes who have never seen a hospital room except when they go for their yearly colonoscopy. They have no idea how hard nursing can be. But that's not what gets me - the thing that gets me is they don't even care how hard the staff has it, what challenges people are facing. They just don't care enough to be bothered."

I just nod. I got that sense, too. Over the intercom, I hear a voice call a code blue on Four East.

Henrietta groans. "That's my unit, Love. Gotta go! Catch up soon, yeah?"

"Code blue? What does that mean?" I ask as Henrietta hastily wraps up her half-eaten lunch.

"It means someone's heart has stopped beating," she says nonchalantly. Is this a common thing? It probably is common in her world, which seems so strange. I quickly hand her a business card, she takes it and runs down the hall. She's leaving her lunch break to save someone's life and I'm here just sending out a couple of random emails and getting paid well to do it.

My head keeps throbbing. I send another email to Hal letting him know that my meeting went well with the administration team. *That's a gross exaggeration of events.* I also tell him he will have my plan tomorrow. Normally, he would insist on having it by the end of the day, but I'm not about to make a promise I can't keep. Besides, he owes me some slack after his obtuse behavior yesterday.

I need to start on my plan soon, even if I don't have to have it done today. Historically Hal has always been my ally. He always pushes me to get things done, but we work as a team to do it. Since I started these healthcare contracts, his behavior has been more demanding. *It's not like he's been doing his part to help me out, either.*

I leave the hospital and drop off my laptop in my hotel room. It's late afternoon. If I take a nap now I'll be off schedule for days. Instead, I walk around downtown for a while.
The fresh air and busy streets invigorate me. I stop for groceries and grab a few easy meals and snacks. On my way to the register, I impulsively grab dark chocolate-covered almonds and a bottle of kombucha, my favorite treats. I immediately regret shopping while hungry. I've overbought and struggle to carry my groceries to my

hotel. I put my groceries away in the kitchenette, hang up my clothes, and set up my desk space the way I like it.

My bed is just a plain, simple hotel bed, but it looks inviting all the same. I ignore it and sit at my newly organized desk space. *I wonder how long I'll stay here before I'm randomly transferred elsewhere.* I need to organize some things in Charleston. I left there so abruptly that no one knows I'm even gone. *No one but Eugene.* I can picture the hint of sadness in his eyes just before he left. I groan and lay my head on my desk. I tell myself leaving Charleston was for the best. The chemistry I have with Eugene was too intense not to pass beyond friendship given enough time. By enough time I mean about 30 more seconds than we had together. Probably less. I shake my head to refocus my thoughts back to work.

I send Helen an email with an itinerary of virtual meetings and agendas to get her nursing recruitment off the ground running. I love doing that sort of thing and I hate that I'm not there to do it in person.

I send Eugene something similar. He must call me as soon as he's done reading it.

"Miss Workaholic, why are you being so formal?" He's trying to imitate my voice and it's just awful, but hilarious at the same time. "Mr. Spinner, I do hope you find these agendas are adequate to prepare you for our weekly meetings. I want them to be a productive use of time."

I laugh and spin my chair around so I can prop my bare feet up on the bed. "It's just a standard blurb I always use. What's wrong with it?"

"I just get the standard blurb? Ouch."

"Yes, via work email you get the standard blurb. Sorry to disappoint," I chuckle.

"You wound me, milady. You made it to New Orleans?"

"Yeah, my flight was delayed and then I had an early morning meeting, so I haven't slept. I'm running on fumes." I lay my head back against the seat and wonder what it would be like if I had stayed in Charleston. I also wonder what it would be like to crawl in bed. *Both are equally tempting.*

"Well, since you haven't been able to sleep, I can accept the standard blurb. I wanted to check in, but I also need to see if we can move my meeting time on Friday."

We make alternate arrangements. I don't have any plans yet so I can accommodate his schedule easily. I'm happy he called and we have a light-hearted conversation. Things were so tense when we said goodbye. Was that just last night?

I hear Eugene take a deep breath. "Vivian, before I go I just want to say something that's totally none of my business. But since we've established we're friends, maybe it's just a little bit my business…"

I interrupt him, knowing where he's going. "I already established boundaries with Hal. Told him that this sort of behavior wouldn't be tolerated."

"I'm glad. You deserve much better than that. But are you sure you want to work for a guy like that? I imagine you have lots of options."

I feel like I don't really have any other options at all, but I don't say it. "Well, since you asked, I'd like to see the guy take an early retirement."

Eugene laughs. "Okay. I'm sure you can handle him just fine. Speaking of retirement, James in HR is retiring early next year. I know it's probably a crazy pay cut for you, but you would be a great HR Director. Our admin team already loves you; you'd be a shoo-in."

"Is he? He wasn't my biggest fan after the stapler incident video I sent him..." For just a moment I consider it. I'd have a home base. Fairly close to my sister. Very close to Eugene...

I shake my head. Those kinds of thoughts aren't productive. I have a job, a boss who has apologized and things are going well. Really well, maybe on the brink of a promotion to Lead Consultant. The promotion would give me a home base and I wouldn't have to take a pay cut. *I can do this, I just need to stick to my plan.*

Eugene interrupts my inner monologue. "You should give it some thought. I like having you around, ya know?"

I like being around. That's a really weird feeling to have. I play with my pen as I think. Would I be happy in one location? Would I be happy with the same people around all the time? "I don't know how to explain this exactly, but Hal was the first person to see me as a person. Someone worthwhile. Outside my family, anyway."

His reply is immediate. "I'm sure others saw you as worthwhile. How could they not?"

"No. No, they didn't. During high school and college, I was the quiet, weird kid that no one wanted around. But working for Hal, things are different. He's been a mentor. He sees me as someone worth investing his time in. That gives me the confidence to do my job. I know most of my interactions with people are only a charade. People just spend time with me because it benefits their goals."

"Maybe some. But not me, milady."

I wonder if it's possible his words are true. They ring true, but how could I ever be sure? My answer is elusive, yet accurate. "Things have always been different with you, Eugene."

He laughs, "Thanks. I think? Sorry, to cut this short, but I've got to run. Duty calls; it's been a hectic day. Don't be a stranger, okay?"

"I can't be a stranger; we have a meeting on Friday. Chat soon, Eugene." I hang up and smile. I need to stick to my work goals. I can't have any distracting entanglements.

Maybe romance isn't in the cards, but it might be feasible to keep Eugene around as a friend. I should be able to keep a friend or two around, even with my hectic work schedule. I need all the allies I can get.

I turn my phone on silent and sit on my balcony. It's got a nice view and the sunshine warms me. I need to take a daily screen break, preferably in the sun. I pull out a snack from my grocery store run to absently munch on it as I filter through the thoughts in my mind. I use this time to allow myself to sort through the thoughts that I've been avoiding.

I dealt with depression during my college years and found a couple of different coping mechanisms that help. My favorite one is going for a run, but my exhaustion prevents that today. I'll have to opt for journaling my feelings instead. I sigh. I know my mental health has taken a hit in the last 24 hours. I don't want to do it. *I need to address all the emotions competing for my headspace.* It will help me rest peacefully and find the ability to focus on New Orleans.

I grab my legal pad and favorite pen.

- *How far away am I from my promotion? Can I keep this pace going?*
- *I need to be a better sister. What does that look like?*
- *I want to go back to Charleston. I don't want to be here.*
- *Is it Charleston I want to return to? Or do I want to return to Eugene?*

I look at my list. *I want to throw things.*

This isn't helping as much as it usually does. Since I lack the energy for a run, I go for another walk to further clear my head. This walk is a time for self-reflection. Self-reflection is for honesty, even if it hurts.

First, my career. Typically Hal has treated me reasonably well, but he was more grumpy and demanding in Charleston. Maybe that was due to the new challenge of healthcare. Since I'm getting a bonus, it wouldn't hurt to stockpile some money in case things get worse. Or maybe I'll want to take an extended leave after this assignment. *Not that I can ever get vacation time approved.*

I take a deep breath. That feels good. Saving up for a rainy day is always a good plan. I owe it to my future self to have a cash reserve, just as a backup.

Next list item: be a better sister. I've not been a bad sister. However, before Charleston, I always avoided any depth of my relationship with Lily. I've started to open up more, and she seems to appreciate getting to know me. It's been good for me, too. She's always been an open book. I make a mental note to call her tomorrow.

Next item: Charleston made me a better version of myself. I'm not sure what happened. Maybe it was being around people who dealt with life-and-death situations as part of their workflow that brought perspective to my life. While I was there I ate better, exercised regularly, and got adequate sleep. I didn't use manipulation as a tool for achieving my goals, for the most part. I genuinely wanted to give the people I was working with something better than their current situation. I enjoyed my work there, it was more fulfilling than my other assignments.

I'm not sure I gave them something better, though. I think Helen is better off - she was an excellent placement. Is Ada better off? Terrance? Would Lucas be if he decides to return? Doubtful. Is Eugene better off?

Eugene. Ugh. There's no sense in denying I'm drawn to him. It's like he has this magnetic pull on me - like nothing I've ever experienced. But there's also no sense in dwelling on the possibility of something more. I can't go there. My work won't let me go there. My career makes me a gypsy. Even if he wanted a long-distance relationship, that isn't feasible since I work seven days a week most of the time. I am hopeful that we can stay friends. Anything beyond friendship is too impractical.

I wander the city streets. It's 7:30 p.m. when I get back to the hotel. I make a cup of hot tea. If I stay up just a bit longer, I'd be on a good schedule by tomorrow. I decide to call my sister tonight since I don't know what tomorrow brings. Lily answers immediately.

"Hey! I'm so happy to hear from you! How's New Orleans?"

I groan. *The sleep deprivation is making me dramatic.* "I don't want to be here. I liked Charleston. How's my apartment working out? Looks like you can keep it as an office even longer, without me being around and interfering."

"I hate hearing that, but I do love your apartment! It's so quiet! I wouldn't mind your interference. You know that. I wish you were around more. I miss you."

I smile. *She's too good to me.* "I miss you. You can have the apartment. For now, anyway."

"For now? Considering a career change!?" she asks excitedly.

"No, nothing like that. But I am increasing my savings. I feel like I need a nest egg just in case. Isn't that the adult thing to do?"

"It is, but I always felt like being an adult was overrated. I wish you were still on the East Coast. I liked you in Charleston. You were close and you seemed healthier and happier than you usually are on assignments."

"Do you know why that is?" I ask. I stand up and pace my hotel room. I'm so sleepy, but it helps to keep moving.

"No. Do you?"

"I'm trying to figure it out." I've done too much soul-searching today. *I need to go back to bottling up my feelings.*

"Is it Charleston you miss? Or Mr. Charleston?"

I give a candid answer. "Both. I think."

"Woah…wait a moment. I thought you and Mr. Charleston were just friends. Are you admitting to having real, actual feelings for him? This feels kind of epic."

Epic? Really? This is exactly why I'm typically evasive with my sister: she tends to blow things out of proportion. But I need to talk this through. She's annoying but good at perspective. "Don't be all weird about it but, yeah. I think I do. It's new to me; I don't understand it. Besides, it's just not practical."

"Practical is never fun. Do you miss Mr. San Diego?"

I was in San Diego about a year ago. I had a short fling with a guy named Todd. We both knew it was short-term. I haven't thought of him since. "No."

"Nothing happened? With Eugene? You were just friends?"

"He was flirtatious and affectionate. He's probably that way with everyone. He gives nice hugs. But nothing more than that, no."

Lily asks, "How did he say goodbye?"

I'm not sure that it matters. But I say, "He said he was gonna miss me. Whispered it in my ear. Gave me a hug."

"Intimate. Interesting. Although. If he wanted something more, that was his window to say something. And yours."

"You read too many romance novels." But she's got a point. I downplayed just how intimate our goodbye was, but maybe I read things wrong. I don't think so. I'm pretty sure he was gonna kiss me goodbye until I pulled away and inadvertently friend-zoned him. I *needed* to friend-zone him. Romance is a distraction I can't deal with right now. Things will be different after I'm promoted. *Different as in Eugene will have moved on and I will have ostracized everyone I care about because I chose work over them.* Woah. Where did that thought come from? I bottle it up where it belongs.

"Vivian, I say this as someone who loves you. Do you just need some friends? Is that what you miss from Eugene?"

I do need friends. She's not wrong. "Yeah. Maybe."

"Do you want advice? You know, from a meddling older sister?"

I chuckle. "Yeah. I think I do."

"Make friends. Connect with people. Men, women, it doesn't matter. Keep it platonic. If you need a friend, that will fill the void. If you need Eugene, the longing will still be there."
I'm beginning to wonder why she's in finance when clearly she should be a life coach. "That's kinda brilliant."

"I am brilliant. What can I say?"

"Sis?" I hesitate to ask this next question, but I do anyway. Fatigue has unblocked my usual filters. "What if I find out the longing is still there, but Eugene has moved on?"

"Hon, it's a risk. Everything worth having in life is a risk. Give yourself a few days. If that question still plagues you, then I'd say you already know what you need to know. My guess is you already do."

"How on Earth did you and Jonathon get together? You used to adamantly avoid any relationship that was close to serious." I was away at college when my sister met Jonathon. They were engaged and married in less than a year.

"Simple. The fear of losing him was greater than the fear of keeping him around."

That doesn't seem even remotely simple. "Why? Why be scared of keeping him around?"

Lily pauses to think here, I assume. "It's hard to say. The act of falling in love is so consuming. It changes everything about your life. Some of the changes are subtle, some less so. I was afraid I would lose myself if I became part of a couple. I was wrong. Being with the right person makes me more of myself, not less. No one before Jonathon was worth the risk of changing."

I mean to keep this thought in my head, but it comes tumbling out anyway. "I don't know how I could have a real relationship with anyone. Something that might last more than just a few weeks."

"Long distance is a challenge. Would it be hard? No doubt. Would it be worth it? Only you can answer that."

Long distance might work if I had any kind of time off. The weekend I took off in Charleston was a rarity. *Normally, I don't have that luxury.* At most, I take a week or so off every three months. Not enough time to sustain a relationship. We hang up and I'm feeling better. Plus it's 8:05 p.m. and I can go to bed now. I'm craving the reset of a good night's sleep. Just because I know it will make her happy, I forward her the picture of Eugene and me at Fort Sumter.

She immediately texts back:

> It's obvious why you would miss him. He's gorgeous. You look gorgeous too. Happy. Love your smile.

Friendship

CHAPTER
20

I quietly slip into a deep and restful sleep. My mind is at peace, at least for the moment. When I finally do wake up, I realize I slept through my alarm and have three missed calls from Hal and one from Henrietta. I call Henrietta first.

"Hey Love, I'm gonna make good on my promise to help you. I know Dr. Stanner. Nice guy. Has a private practice nearby with several other physicians. They've decided to close it down - all the docs are near retirement age and are ready to live out their golden years in peace. They're good people. They don't want their nurses unemployed. The practice is paying them severance, I think, but he wants them taken care of long-term. I have a lunch meeting set up for today with the entire practice."

Henrietta is officially the best person ever. "I'm coming with you. I can order lunch."

"I was hoping you'd say that. I was hoping you'd run the meeting. It's 12, maybe 15, nurses. It was a big practice."

"I can run the meeting, sure. Text me the address. It's time to recruit!" I send Hal an email about my plan to recruit these nurses and tell him I've already scheduled a security audit. I can call later when I have more to update.

Hoping that appeases him for a while, I shower and have lunch ordered. I remember these bath bombs my sister raves about, so I pick up those and some other self-care items. I have a suitcase full of marketing things that I didn't use in Charleston. Just the usual. Pens, tote bags, sticky notes. I'm using them now. I don't want to haul these items through another airport, if for no other reason. I get to the clinic early to set up the table of goodies and ensure lunch is on time.

Henrietta comes in and starts laughing. "You come in with guns blazing. I love it! Remember what you said about nurses being irreplaceable? I'm not here to tell you how to do your job, but if it were me, that's where I'd start."

The staff starts filing in and they have the "what is she selling" attitude; mostly I don't blame them. I move quickly before people are even settled.

"My name is Vivian Ashmead with Aberlin Consulting. I'm not one of you. I can't start an IV. I can't hold the hand of someone who is dying. I would freak out. If someone in this room has a heart that stops beating, I am by far the least helpful. I'm not sure I can even manage a call to 911."

That gets a couple of chuckles.

"What I am is an Employee Retention and Recruitment Specialist. I'm good at my job and Lake Pontchartrain Hospital has hired me. They need my help. But the lunch and the goodies? That's not a bribe. That's to thank you. To thank you for what you do. I've spent the last few weeks talking with nurses. I know it's not easy. I know the pandemic made it even worse. If you want to, take your lunch and swag and go about your day. That's totally fine. You are not a captive audience. But before you leave, I want to express my gratitude."

I wait. Henrietta arches an eyebrow at me. It's a bold move, sure. A couple of nurses leave. Most stay.

"The hospital I represent is not without its issues. Henrietta can attest to that, no doubt." She nods her head in agreement.

I continue, "I'm here to make things better. I've already told the hospital administration that they need to treat nurses like they're irreplaceable. Because they are. You are. I need to help the hospital expand its team. I've scheduled a security audit so we can make changes to ensure staff safety. I'll be working with individual departments to troubleshoot issues and make the hospital a place nurses want to work, nurses like you. I won't interrupt your lunch further. But I will be here to answer any questions you might have."

Henrietta looks at me like I've grown a third arm. But nearly every nurse left wants a job, or at least an interview. I start collecting contact information and making a list of nurses looking for employment. If I can secure even half of these nurses, it'll be a huge step towards my goals.

We're putting away the lunch leftovers when Henrietta says, "I would've never played it like that, Love. You didn't even try to sell it; yet they came anyway. Color me amazed."

I shrug. "The one thing I've learned from when I was in Charleston is that nurses want to be nurses. They just need some support."

Henrietta smiles and tucks an unruly black curl of hair behind her ear. "True statement. I took off the afternoon to go to a couple of consignment stores. What are you up to?"

What am I up to? Like I have options. "Just work."

Henrietta starts counting on her fingers. "You just recruited, like ten nurses. I still can't believe it. Wanna take a break? Tag along? I'm sure you usually shop in fancy stores…"

"Are you kidding? I love thrifting! I usually shop at thrift stores so I can frequently update my wardrobe and pack light. You don't mind company?"

Henrietta squeals. "No! I'd love you to come! This is gonna be fun. But I walked here - I live close by. I gotta go grab my car."

"My rental car is here. I can drive if you can navigate."

"Deal."

I start driving to our first thrift store. She's so easy to talk to, it feels like I've known her forever. I find out she's from a military family who moved frequently and now she doesn't know how to set down roots. It's a feeling that resonates with me. She's been in New Orleans for a couple of years. She's having boyfriend issues and wonders if it's time to move on.

"Maybe it's a sign? Maybe I'm just a gypsy at heart."

She's wearing a beautiful silk headband and maybe could pass for an actual gypsy. "I should be trying to make you stay right here; that's what I've been hired to do. But I do have contacts in Charleston if that's where you land. I can easily get you a job there. "

"I remember you saying you weren't ready to leave Charleston. What makes you miss it, Love?"

I initially avoid the question as we get out and walk into our first store. But then, I remember Lily's advice to make friends and Henrietta just told me half her life story on the way over. I absently start looking through the clothing rack. "Not sure what exactly I miss about Charleston. It might be a who? Though I do love downtown Charleston and being near the ocean."

She grins widely. "Ohhhh, now you gotta tell me this bit of gossip. Thrifting and gossip make my day."

I struggle with how exactly to describe Eugene. *Stupidly perfect?* I pull out my phone and show her the picture of me and Eugene from Fort Sumter. Our only one. I wish I had more.
"Good heavens, look at those arms, Love. Defined, but not bulky gym rat. You have good taste. Gotta tell ya, I wouldn't mind being wrapped up in those arms."

Yeah. Me, too. I think of our last lingering embrace. Just a breath away from…more. I just shrug. "His name is Eugene. He gives good hugs."

She smiles wickedly. "My guess is that he's good at more than just *hugs*."

He likely is, but I try to block the mental images those thoughts conjure. *I'm not successful. Oh boy.* "We're just friends. I wouldn't know."

Henrietta shakes her head and hands me back my phone. "That's a shame. You want more?"

I toss my phone back in my bag. "He's a work contact. So that's tricky. I have a strict policy with keeping things professional with work contacts."

She nods. "Fraternizing at work is messy. Believe me, I know."

I tilt my head.

She shakes her head no. "Nope. That's a story for another day. Let's just say making out with a co-worker Grey's-Anatomy-style in an empty stairwell makes work complicated."

I laugh. "Like the show, 'Grey's Anatomy'? I didn't know that ever really happened!"

She gives me a knowing look. "It happens more than you'd think. So your boy is off limits because he's a work contact? I get that. But how long is he a work contact? It's not like you're still in Charleston. Does he want more?"

I keep moving through the aisles of the store. I've never made friends easily, but I feel like I can tell Henrietta anything. "I think he might want more, but I don't know. He's never said so. But yeah. Maybe on some level, I do want more. Things are different with Eugene. It's not just attraction. He isn't annoying to talk to. I like hanging out with him. I usually steer clear of anything that isn't short-term. Not many people want a partner that's gone more than they're home."

She looks at me sympathetically. "Ah, I get it. He's too important to you to be a fling. He means too much. But the real deal? That's a scary leap, Love. Believe me, I know."

I look at her, astonished. I've been wracking my brain about this for 48 hours now and she hits the nail on the head in a couple of minutes. Not that it matters anyway. I could never make that leap, even if I wanted to. It wouldn't be fair to Eugene.

It's time for a subject change. Fast. "What happened with your boyfriend? If you don't mind me asking."

"Ethan. Tall, dark, and dreamy. Approached me using his Cajun accent. I've made many a bad decision because someone spoke to me with a magnificent accent. Gets me every single time. Eugene has an accent?"

I blush a bit as I think of how Eugene says "milady" as if he's never been in a hurry in his entire life. "He does. Not quite Southern - it's hard to describe."

"It's the Charleston accent. Unique to that area. It's a posh twist on Southern. The accent gets you, too." Henrietta smiles.

The accent. The arms. The fact that he's not annoying. It all gets me. "It does."

"Guy-from-the-stairwell-make-out-sessions had a Boston accent. I love that accent; it's like the letter 'R' never existed. The accent is my demise every time. If I ever meet someone British I'm in trouble. That accent is my favorite." Henrietta shakes her head and I chuckle.

"Anyway, Ethan popped the question. Proposed to me in the French Quarter. I thought we were getting beignets." She runs her hands through her curls. Somehow they spring back to where they are supposed to be.

I raise my eyebrows. "And?"

Henrietta talks with her hands, they flail wildly around. "That fool! It came out of nowhere! We've had exactly zero discussions about marriage. He'd never even said 'I love you' before that night."

"What did you do?!" I've been holding the same top for several minutes. I forgot we were shopping.

"I told that fool no. Broke up with him on the spot. That's not how things are done."

"Wow…" I'm not sure how else to answer that. It seems like marriage might be more trouble than it's worth.

"So it kinda messed with my head. I'm wondering if I need a change of scenery."

"When did all this go down?" I ask. *Henrietta's life could be a best-selling novel. Maybe even a movie.*

Henrietta takes a deep breath. "Just a couple of weeks ago. The fool calls me every night. I've never answered. I haven't spoken to him since that night."

Ethan is persistent. "Would it be worth a conversation? Maybe you could find closure?"

She smirks at me. "You gonna tell Eugene how you feel? Isn't that worth a conversation?"

I shake my head before I answer. "Touché."

We both laugh. It feels so good to laugh. Time for another subject change. "What's it like, being a nurse?"

Henrietta furrows her brow "Girl, that's work."

"Not really, I mean what does it mean to you? Personally? It's more than a job?"

"Nurses are people who wanna fix things. Sometimes, there are problems we can't fix. Some people are not gonna get better. Some have awful home situations. The thing is, the good has to outweigh the bad. That's how you keep going. The good barely tipped the scales before COVID. The pandemic made everything in healthcare worse. So that's a problem. I try to point out the good and focus on the good for me and my team. But there's lots of bad out there to contend with, Love. Lots." She looks suddenly burdened.

I pick up a saucepan to use while I'm here so I can avoid eating out so much. "Is that why nurses are leaving healthcare?"

She shrugs. "Some of them, yeah. It just got to be too much. Don't get me wrong, being a nurse has its rewarding moments. It keeps you going when things are hard."

I smile at her. *Did I make a friend? It feels like it.* "I admire the ability to push through the bad and find the good. Not many people can do that."

"Yesterday, I had a patient who underwent a scoliosis repair. The surgeon put two long rods in her spine. Prior to surgery, she couldn't sit up straight due to the severe curve of her spine. It was bad enough to cause pain, digestion, and even breathing issues. She's 17 years old, just a kid. I went in with the Physical Therapist. The PT helped her sit on the side of the bed. She sat upright - tall and proud for the first time. She caught a glimpse of herself in the mirror and started to cry. She looked normal, like any other 17-year-old kid, minus surgical scars on her back. She had happy tears, Love. It was a magical moment."

Henrietta and I shop a bit longer. She's funny, caring, and incredibly insightful. *I can't imagine a better person as a friend.* I had the most fun thrift shopping that I've had in a long time. Or ever. I drop her back off at home. As she gets out of the car she exclaims "Girl, we gotta do this again!"

For the next few weeks, I buckle down and settle into a routine. I interview and recruit nurses. Despite my shaky meeting with the administration early on, things are going remarkably well. I work with management on team building and staff retention. I've been able to recruit several nurses and have strengthened connections with universities so they can hire new graduates.

I also make time for thrift shopping with Henrietta. I chat with Eugene and Lily. My life has more meaning and is more fulfilling than it has been in a long time. *But I do miss something.* I have a subtle, underlying loneliness that doesn't seem to ever completely dissolve. The unfortunate paradox is that the more I build real relationships with people, the more lonely I become.

I dedicate Fridays to Charleston. But really, things are going pretty well without me. Helen's a machine. She's hiring from all around the state.

Helen's marketing idea of pitching Charleston as a wonderful place to live is quite successful. The hospital has already ended over half its traveling nurse contracts, which offsets the cost of the security audit and my consulting fees. Talking to Helen is always fun, too. We'll be in the middle of discussing nurse retention and she goes off-topic and tells me her favorite recipe. Then back to work again.

Eugene is doing great with his staff and we agreed to decrease our work meetings to monthly. On the friendship side of things, we chat all the time. It's the highlight of my week. We discuss everything. The weather. All of his hobbies. My thrift store finds. Politics. Books and movies. Hopes and dreams. *When has the highlight of my week been something that isn't work-related? I can't even remember.*

Late at night I replay conversations with Eugene in my head and then try to convince myself not to read too much into it. *It's my own special type of torture.* Why I would do this to myself when I've already mentally friend-zoned him, I will never know.

I'm gonna miss you, Vivian Ashmead…

I like having you around, ya know…

One night when my mind is spinning too much and I can't sleep, I send Eugene a text. I hadn't heard from him all day. Just a simple 'I hope you had a good day' text. It's late so I don't expect a response. But I get one when he immediately calls.

"Why are you up so late, Miss Workaholic?"

I stretch out across the bed. "You're on Eastern time - it's even later there."

He groans. "I know; I can't sleep."

"Everything okay?" I ask. I know he's not okay, I can hear it in his voice.

He hesitates a moment. "Just a hard day at work."

I get the feeling he doesn't want to talk about it. I push a little anyway. "You want to tell me about it? Maybe it will help to talk it out."

He takes a deep breath. "I covered the trauma unit today. Priscilla usually covers it, but she's on vacation this week. I've been in the trauma unit before. You kind of have to mentally detach yourself from what's going on. Trauma can be pretty horrific."

"Was it today? Horrific?"

"Yeah. I had a 19-year-old GSW, T10 compete."

I roll my eyes. "In English, Eugene."

He chuckles. "Sorry. It's a habit. It means the kid got shot in the spine during an armed robbery. He's completely paralyzed from the waist down."

I gasp and sit straight up in bed. "He's only 19 years old?!"

"Yeah. He was in the wrong place at the wrong time. He asked me if he would ever walk again. I answered honestly and told him no. He knew the answer on some level already, though the docs had been sugarcoating things. He's doing okay, considering. It's just..." he trails off and doesn't finish.

"Horrific?" I ask, wishing I could take some of his pain.

"Yeah. Horrific. And it got to me."

"Of course it did, you're only human. You're a good human. How could it not get to you?" My heart squeezes with pain for the guy who lost the ability to walk at such a young age.

It hurts for Eugene who has a front-row seat to tragedy as part of his normal work day. My chest feels tight and I remind myself to breathe.

"I guess so." He yawns. "I wish you were here, milady."

I lay back down and settle under my blanket. "I miss being in Charleston," I say. It's late and my defenses are down. I also admit, "I miss you, too, Eugene."

"Do you?" he asks. Not in his typical tone of ridiculous flirtation. He sounds almost hopeful.

"Yeah, I do. No one else calls me 'milady' or 'Miss Workaholic' here. It's so weird."

He laughs."if that isn't a good enough reason for you to come back to Charleston, I don't know what is."

"I mean, you're not wrong." The longing for Charleston seems stronger than ever tonight. I thought it might fade with time.

"If you were here, we could call in sick tomorrow and I'd take you to another cheesy tourist attraction. Maybe your idiot boss wouldn't interfere this time."

It's the first time either of us has mentioned Fort Sumter. I want to say more. Like, I'm sorry I accidentally friend-zoned you, I didn't mean to. Except maybe I did mean to because work was whisking me away. I thought it'd be easier to say goodbye to him as friends. Plus a real relationship, not just a short-term fling, is not at all practical. Friend-zoning was the responsible thing to do. I always do the responsible thing. *Sometimes being an adult is stupid.* I leave all of that unsaid, but it stays in my mind, swirling around.

Eugene chuckles. "I can almost hear you overthinking…"

I'm indignant. "You can not."

He laughs even more. Then he challenges, "What's going on in your head, then?"

I ignore the question. "I don't overthink. Much."

Eugene chuckles again. *Clearly, I am a terrible liar.* I need to get off the phone before I admit something I can't walk back. Instead, I sigh wistfully. "I was just thinking, that does sound perfect. Maybe one day. Good night, Eugene."

"Sweet dreams, milady."

I fall asleep and my dreams are indeed sweet. But they're just dreams and in reality, what I want seems so far out of reach.

I wake up the next morning, seriously considering taking Eugene's idea and calling in sick. Work is going well enough, so there's no reason to. But the thought lingers in my mind, a sick day is something I never do. Even when I'm actually sick.

I call Hal to update him; he's grumpy, but not overly so. I don't think I'm needed much longer in New Orleans. I discuss this with Hal but he wants me to stay here for two more weeks and try to recruit a few more nurses. He gives no indication of where my next steps lie. I mention that I could go back to Charleston and do a short follow-up visit. He immediately shoots that down, reminding me that he gave me a bonus so I could move on from Charleston.

He's probably right. I should move on from Charleston, professionally speaking. My mind tends to wander to Charleston with an alarming frequency. I can't seem to shake it off.

The problem with staying two more weeks in New Orleans is that I don't have enough to do to make it worthwhile. With Henrietta's help, we've recruited several nurses. I've also worked with department heads on retention goals. I'll be meeting with a few of them long-term to monitor progress; there's no real way to speed that up. Otherwise, everyone has been fairly receptive to my input. Security measures are being added. Some policies have been updated or changed. Over time, word will get out that the hospital is a decent place to work. They will earn the reputation that they value their staff. That's the best way of building and maintaining adequate personnel.

Since I don't have a ton of other things to work on, I go back to recruiting nurses who have recently left. I schedule a meeting with Casey, a nurse who recently resigned from the emergency department. The hospital wants her to return. She was a well-loved Charge Nurse. Word has it, the ED ran like a well-oiled machine with Casey at the helm. I meet her at a coffee shop and she tells me immediately she's not coming back.

Of course. *Fantastic.* I try to mask my irritation, but it doesn't work. "Why even agree to meet with me, then?"

She sits down with a coffee. "I want you to know about my friend. I want you to know that nurses aren't lying. They aren't exaggerating. Maybe you wield enough power to help us."

That's flattering, but also quite doubtful. "What happened?"

"She was working at a neighboring hospital, Downtown. A patient brutally assaulted her. Multiple injuries. Multiple surgeries. She was there trying to help him and he nearly killed her." Casey's whole body is tense.

I know about this incident. It was an isolated one, but I imagine it doesn't feel isolated when it's a friend. "How is she now?"

She shakes her head. "Awful. She can't work. She's on disability. She's depressed."

"I heard about it on the news. I hate that it happened to her. That shouldn't happen to anyone. Surely she has some PTSD from it? Is she getting the help she needs?"

"She's working through some things; she's getting professional help. But, look - you just can't erase experiencing that kind of trauma. You live with it, but it's always there lurking in the shadows. It haunts her."

Casey pauses for a minute here and I wait patiently. I know I can't get her back. Normally, when I realize I'm not getting anywhere, I wrap things up immediately. Move on to more productive tasks. But I've gotten lost in her story and can't walk away. I don't have anything more pressing, anyway.

I take a sip of my coffee so I have a moment to gather my thoughts. "Casey, I know the nurses aren't lying. I believe every word you're telling me. One of my main objectives has been to upgrade security measures."

"When you talk to important people, remember my friend. Remember this is what society thinks of nurses. Of any healthcare worker. The ones we're dedicated to serve may very well be the ones that kill us." Her eyes shine with unshed tears, her love and concern for her friend apparent. She stands up and leaves without further conversation.

I watch her walk away and don't stop her from leaving. I wonder what important people she thinks I can talk to. I don't have the influence she needs. To think, when I took this job I thought I would single-handedly save healthcare. Well, maybe not healthcare overall, but at least the places where I'm sent. I have never been so naive.

I call Hal, though I hate to do it. I've been trying to communicate via email as much as possible. We aren't far into our conversation and he's angry. I mean, he's livid.

Hal curses under his breath. "You were supposed to get Casey back. That was a top priority of our contract with them. This is your job, Viv! To get these nurses back to work."

"I've gotten nurses back to work, both in Charleston and in New Orleans. I won't get all of them back. You know we never get everyone back that we try to recruit. It doesn't matter if we don't get this one specific nurse; we got others." I'm hoping if I can get Hal to just objectively look at the numbers, he can't help but be reasonable. No such luck. I'm beginning to think Hal set me up for failure by not insisting on a budget to increase salaries. However, my success, or lack thereof, reflects on him. He wouldn't sabotage things.

"But they wanted *this* nurse, Viv. I hired you to do what needs to be done. Get her back. You were able to get Chad Fitzgerald back to WindyCity."

"Hal, I could increase Chad's salary!" *Not to mention sitting on his lap and making promises I wasn't going to keep.*

I still feel some shame about that level of manipulation. Was getting Chad back worth it? Either way, I can't imagine that scenario would play out the same with Casey.

"Viv…"

I interrupt and continue, "She said no. She has a right to say no. It's her life. I cannot dictate her choices. That's not how this works. Casey isn't coming back: there's no sense in pursuing it further. It's not going to happen. If I could offer more money then maybe I could get somewhere."

"You really are a disappointment, Kid."

I try to ignore that statement. *But RUDE.* "Her best friend was brutally assaulted *on the job. By a patient.* Surely you could see why she'd be hesitant to return."

"I don't get it. I'll never understand why poor people don't want to work."

"She's not poor. She's middle class. That has nothing to do with this. Even if she pulled a six-figure salary she doesn't deserve to be brutally assaulted." I hold the phone with one hand and rub my temple with the other. This whole conversation is pointless.

"I've seen nurses' salaries. They're poor. Yet, they keep leaving their work. I don't understand it." Hal grumbles something else about "poor people" that I don't fully catch. I don't care. *His behavior is grating on my nerves today.*

"I'll never understand why essential personnel get paid so little. This woman knows how to restart a heart that's stopped beating. She knows what medicines will help and which are more likely to harm. It's a huge responsibility for the pay they receive." I stop the cat-like pacing I usually do when I talk to Hal and sit down. This conversation is sucking the life out of me like air from a balloon.

Hal continues to mutter under his breath. "How very philosophical. I don't pay you to make excuses, I pay you to get things done. Pack your things - change of plans. I'm sending you to Nashville. I'll have my assistant send flight details."

He hangs up before I can defend myself. Too philosophical? A disappointment because I couldn't get one recruit back? My numbers look pretty good for Charleston and even better for New Orleans. Especially for a new assignment where we're just trying to learn the lay of the land. Surely he can't expect things to go as well as technology assignments. We've been doing those for *years.* I have money as an enticement. I cannot believe he's hung up on this one nurse.

This is nothing like my robotics assignment in Chicago. I don't get why Hal can't seem to see the difference.

I check my email and fortunately, my flight is tomorrow night. I'm happy to not have to rush around. I text Henrietta to let her know it's my last night in town and to ask her to dinner. She agrees to an early dinner since she has a morning shift tomorrow.

We're sitting in the restaurant and after we order our food Henrietta slaps my arm and says, "I can't believe you're leaving, Love. Who's gonna keep me company with thrift shopping and gossip?"

I give her a sad smile. While I won't miss New Orleans, I am desperately going to miss Henrietta. "Maybe a weekly call to discuss thrift finds? Plus, I have to wrap up a few loose ends here to complete the assignment."

She slumps her shoulders and sighs. "It's not the same. I'm gonna work a few more months in New Orleans. But if I'm still itching to go, maybe Charleston is calling my name. Can you still get me a good job there?

I smile and allow myself a quick moment to dream of Charleston. "Of course. I wish I could go with you."

She gives me a knowing smirk. "Still missing your boy? You can come with me, Love. We can both go to Charleston."

My 'boy'? Ha. I wonder what Eugene would think of being called "my boy." He'd make a joke of it, no doubt. "You know how my work is. It doesn't let me settle down. Have you talked with Ethan yet?"

She craftily ignores my question, which is her way of saying no. She continues, "Working is a necessity. But working at your current job, it's not a necessity. You can change the narrative, love. Try something new."

That sounds disturbingly similar to something Lily said to me. What if it is my choice? I feel so very depleted. "The work I do now? That's all I know. I've been doing it since I graduated college."

Henrietta frowns at me. "So?"

"So? So I don't know how to change the narrative. I don't have another path. My work is me; I am my work." *Change the narrative. Yeah, right.* It's like she has no idea what that would do to my calendar. Or what it would do to my six-month, one-year, and five-year plans. That, yes, I have outlined in detail.

She reaches over the table and squeezes my arm affectionately. "Look, that's simply not true, and I think you know that deep down. Love, you're so much more than your work. You're a good friend. An incredible advocate. Sounds like you're a good sister. If you give that boy of yours a chance, you would be a good partner, too. I can't think of one thing that you can't do if you set your mind to it."

She's wrong, of course. Work is all I have. She goes to leave and wraps me in a hug I didn't know I was craving. "Henrietta, I'm gonna miss you!" I say. I mean it, too.

She's walking away but stops for a minute. "Vivian, you choose the next chapter of your life. No one else. You write the next page. You choose what happens next. I, for one, can't wait to hear what it's about."

I just smile back at her before I walk away. I try to say something, but the words are stuck beneath the inexplicable lump in my throat. I don't deserve her kindness. Her faith in me? Well, that's unfounded. *I can't just wipe the slate clean and start anew. The very thought of it cripples me with fear. I have to find a way to make things work out at Aberlin. I'm so close to being promoted. Securing the Lead Consultant position would give me so much more freedom and flexibility with assignments. I'm tired of being moved around on someone else's whim.*

Right now I need to wrap my head around this sudden change in plans. If I've been such a disappointment in New Orleans, then why move me to another city?

Loneliness

CHAPTER

23

I'm back at the hotel and a crushing loneliness consumes me. I call Lily, but she doesn't answer. I start packing, but it doesn't distract me. I play music but that does nothing to soothe the ache inside. Somewhere between Hal calling me a disappointment and Henrietta just flippantly saying I could try something new - like it was as easy as trying on a new jacket - my mind is a jumbled mess. I pull out my notebook to write down my thoughts, but I can't find enough clarity.

I scroll through my phone and pull up Eugene's number. I chew my lip as I consider calling. I've never hesitated to call before, but tonight feels different. My conversation with Henrietta has me tied up in knots. I love my job, but it does cost me a lot, too. Friendships. Stability. A home. It's not like Hal's been a gem to work with lately either. I briefly allow myself the thought of living in Charleston. *What would I do? How would that work?*

I get over myself and go out on my hotel balcony to call Eugene. He seems happy to hear from me.

We chat about life and our week. Our friendship has grown, even with me being in New Orleans. Other than Lily, he's my favorite person, not that I would ever say those words out loud. Instead, I tell him I'm heading to Nashville next.

"Want to come back to Charleston for a visit in between assignments? Or I could do a long weekend in Nashville," he suggests. "It would be fun to hang out for a weekend."

Once again I tell myself not to read too much into this, but his words do nothing but cultivate the longing I have inside of me. I could put off starting in Nashville until Monday and go to Charleston for a couple of days. But I'm not sure how I feel about that. So, I lie. "I have to get started right away in Nashville. Let me get settled and see what I can work out, okay?"

"Sure, let me know. Are you looking forward to Nashville?"

"Not really. I don't know why. I usually love the thrill of a new city and a new assignment. I've been moving so quickly the last few months. I still haven't wrapped things up in Charleston. I've got loose ends in New Orleans, and now adding on another location? It's a bit daunting. Plus I haven't been home in months."

Eugene chuckles. "Sounds like you need some time off."

"I'm going to try to take some time after Nashville if I can. Everything's been so urgent with these healthcare assignments that I haven't been able to take off work." That's most likely not true. Hal will probably move me to the next location quickly.

"I don't see why. Healthcare has been a mess for years. It's getting worse, sure. But it's going to take years to fix it, if it's even fixable. Healthcare needs changes at the federal level."

He has a point, though I'm sure Hal would disagree. "Yeah, I get that. I can make small, effective changes at a local hospital. But American healthcare probably needs a complete overhaul. It's not like I can save the whole system."

"If anyone could, my money would be on you, milady."

I roll my eyes. "Eugene, how attached are you to your work? If you couldn't be a physical therapist anymore, where would that leave you?"

"You're asking as a friend, right? Not in a work capacity?"

That's an odd clarification. Does he think I would sabotage his work because of something he told me when we were just chatting? I wouldn't do that to him. I guess even a friendship with a work contact can bring complications. "Yeah, of course. It's a friend question."

"If I won the lottery or inherited a couple million dollars, would I be a PT? Probably not. I might do some occasional pro bono work, I think I'd like that. But for the most part, I have a decent job. My salary pays my bills. I'm better off than many. My identity is not wrapped up in my work though, no. I'm Eugene. I happen to be a PT. If being a PT goes away, I'm still Eugene." He pauses here.

A decent job where he has to tell a kid he'll never walk again. A salary that keeps him in a one-bedroom condo. I hesitate a moment before asking, "Do you like being in management?" I'm not entirely sure I want to know the answer.

Eugene hedges, "I can't seem to find career contentment. It's hard, being a PT. I'm an introvert."

I wonder if that means he doesn't like management. Did I put him in a place that just fosters more discontentment? I didn't mean to do that. I feel a pain in my chest that feels suspiciously like a twinge of guilt.

What was I supposed to do? Hal insisted on progress. At least Eugene is making more money now. I decide to stick with the introvert angle of this conversation. "Are you really? You're so outgoing!"

"Ha, ha. I guess. I can be friendly, sure. But it drains me as the day goes on. I come home from work, I don't want to interact with anyone else, I've hit my quota of people."

I go back into my hotel and stretch out across my bed, although I should finish packing. "You interact with me after work."

"You're, uh…. It's different with you. You don't drain me, milady."

Eugene doesn't drain me, either. "I'm an introvert, too. I feel like much of my work is a game of charades. I thrive doing the behind-the-scenes projects."

"You're more attached to your work? It's more of your identity?"

"Yeah," I admit. "It is. I'm not sure who I am outside of work if I could even exist without my job."

"You'd be fine. You'd be shaken for a while, I imagine. But hear me out, you're strong. You've got a skill set that employers would love. You get things done in a way that's fair and compassionate. You have strong ethics. If your job goes away, you still have those qualities. You would still be Vivian. You'd still be amazing."

I don't have strong ethics and he knows that from our conversation on the boat leaving Fort Sumter. "Amazing? Ha! That's a bit of a stretch. Don't you think?"

Eugene's single-word answer comes without hesitation. "No."

"Eugene..." My voice trails off. What am I supposed to say to that anyway?

"Vivian, I think you're amazing. I'm sure you've realized that by now."

I don't like when Eugene says my name - it always increases the seriousness of his tone. Does he actually think I'm amazing? What does that even mean? Amazing at my job? As a person? I could ask for clarification, but I have no idea what lies down that road. So I do the most logical thing and change the subject. "If I can knock out a few more assignments, I'd be eligible for Lead Consultant."
"Woah. Sounds fancy. What does that mean?" Eugene asks. I may be reading too much into this, but he sounds impressed. Maybe he does think my work is amazing.

"It's a promotion. My boss Hal is a Lead Consultant. If I were one, too, it would allow me the option to hire my own team. It'd be much less traveling; I could have a home base. If I were promoted, I'd be the youngest Lead Consultant at Aberlin. I've put in enough work to justify the promotion at my age."

"Is a home base preferable? Or do you like traveling?"

"I did like traveling, but lately not as much. I feel kind of drained lately." I drag myself off my bed to finish packing.

We chat a little longer but the conversation stays in my head after I hang up the call. I don't know how I ended up with friends that are so good to me, that think so highly of me. It's a kindness I certainly don't deserve. They're not right; I can't just start over - start a new chapter. *Can I?*

As I finish packing to leave New Orleans behind, I contemplate calling Eugene back and telling him I will fly to Charleston for a couple of days. I even check and find out I could easily get a flight. The idea of seeing Eugene makes me uneasy. I need to keep him friend-zoned.
I'm afraid if we share any physical space - if he shows any interest at all - I won't be able to resist his charms again. I barely resisted at Fort Sumter. I sit back on the bed and close my eyes. I wonder what would've happened that night

if I didn't have to leave. I wonder if Eugene and I are a possibility after I'm promoted to Lead Consultant. I'd still have to work long hours, but I would have a home base. I could move to Charleston.

A promotion could still be another year away. Maybe more. I doubt Eugene would just wait on me. Who's to say we're long-term material anyway? I admit we have chemistry. I'd even admit that I care for him. However, he is still a distraction. I need to remember my goals. He isn't one of my goals.

I need to go back to being happy with who I am. In some ways, my sister's advice about making friends backfired - I now feel longing and loneliness more than ever. I'm painfully aware of a gnawing void inside. I never felt loneliness like this before. *Now it seems I can't escape it.*

Nashville

I'm in downtown Nashville, spending a little extra time (the time I could be spending with Eugene if I wasn't such a ninny) setting up my room how I like it and making preparations for this next week. I've requested an extra desk and I picked up three dry erase boards. One for Charleston, one for New Orleans, and one for my current assignment in Nashville. I spend a few hours going through emails and getting organized. Having to manage three separate assignments is ridiculous. Having the visuals of the whiteboards helps; it allows me to focus and prioritize. Even so, I'm having trouble avoiding feeling overwhelmed.

I start by sending out nursing surveys and invitations to people who've recently left and preparing for my meeting with the administration team. I take my slideshow from New Orleans and tweak it a bit, no need to start from scratch.

When I meet with the administration team, I take the same approach as I did in New Orleans, telling them what needs to be done. However, it doesn't go nearly as well.

The team doesn't want a security audit - which is *absurd* - as they have documented increases in violence at their hospital! Not even in the area, but in this specific facility. I've learned a thing or two from the other security audits, so I suggest some changes based on that information. "It won't be specifically tailored to your facilities, but it's better than nothing," I tell them. Reluctantly, they agree. Everything I recommend is a fight and I start to wonder why they hired us in the first place. *Fantastic.*

I leave that meeting fairly annoyed and meet with Alvin, a nurse from the surgical floor who recently left. He echoes some security concerns that I have, but his reason for not returning is due to a back injury.

He shakes his head. "I just can't do it anymore, Vivian. It's too much pain. I'm 34 years old and the doctors say I need major spinal surgery. I can't keep treating my body this way."

I ask him about lift equipment - machines that mechanically move an immobile patient from point A to point B. Alvin tells me the hospital has them, but not enough of them. That's an issue I can fix, but I cannot fix Alvin's spinal injuries. I promise better access to lift equipment for his colleagues.

A genuine smile appears across his face."Thank you!! It's too late to save me from my injuries, but it might not be too late for someone else."

I start to leave and Alvin stops me. "Vivian, my aunt is on the hospital's Board of Directors. They hired your company to make some changes due to an outcry from employees. However, the administration team that you'll work with directly isn't as happy about you being here."

Say what? "Why are you telling me this?"

"I'd prepare for a battle if I were you. Our administration is notorious for putting on a show but doing very little." He shrugs and we say our goodbyes. *Hopefully, he's wrong and the administration team just needs a little encouragement.*

I text Eugene to see if he can give me a run down about lift equipment. I know the general idea, but I need more expert knowledge.

He responds:

> I'd be happy to help. That can be our focus at our Friday meeting. Everything is good here.

Our meetings aren't supposed to be him helping me, but I'm also not going to fight him on that. I'm drowning in work. *I'll take any kind of lifeline.*

I have several meetings with other healthcare workers who have recently resigned and it echoes what I've been hearing elsewhere.

"Too many perverts to deal with…"

"I don't feel safe…"

"I have injuries and pain from assisting patients…"

"I'm tired of being micromanaged…."

"Too much emphasis on the bottom line and not quality of care…"

"Working nights, weekends, and holidays is wreaking havoc on my relationships…"

"If I'm essential, so vital to our society, then where's the compensation? I need more money…"

"Violence in healthcare is rising. I don't want to be a part of it anymore…"

I keep coming up with dead ends but optimistically continue to schedule more interviews. About a week into my assignment in Nashville, I meet Rebecca. She's a nurse who recently left. She's signed up to do substitute teaching in the school system.

"That's got to be hard work," I say. "The pay is less than nursing, too."

She presses her lips together in a thin line. "I needed a break from nursing. Being a substitute is hard, but it's a different kind of hard. Sometimes you just need a change. I know we're short nurses, but the schools are short teachers. You pick and choose. Besides, I don't have to work weekends, holidays, or night shifts as a teaching substitute."

I realize this is the part I don't understand - the need people seem to have for change, the ability to start a new chapter. This theme keeps circling its way back to me. I'm vexed by its recurrence. I doubt I want to know the answer to my next question, but I ask it anyway. "Why did you leave?"

She scowls as if scrolling through some unpleasant memories. "Oh, lots of things. I can tell you the straw that broke the camel's back. I was minding my own business, walking down the hall to check on a patient who had called for me. This man, out of nowhere, cornered me up against the wall. He was shaking his finger in my face and screaming at me. Asking me if I was so stupid to think that masks still work. He was screaming at me! When do we cross the line from verbal to physical violence? The verbal assaults kept escalating. Not just this one random dude. Multiple people. I don't know when those verbal assaults might turn physical, but I'm not going to stick around and find out."

I probably look like an idiot, because I realize my jaw is gaping open. I try several times to say something, but what is there to say? So I just go with a generic, "I'm sorry." It feels like an empty sentiment. I hate that I'm even saying it. I've heard things similar to this on the news, but have been in denial it happens.

As the days drag on, I reluctantly update Hal via email from time to time. I haven't had much success. At all. He doesn't just email me back; he calls so he can yell at me. Tells me to try harder, to do more. Again and again. I continue to be a disappointment. So I try harder, and I disappoint more.
Even getting out of bed to face a new day has become challenging. I've little hope of it being better - success in Nashville seems like a pipe dream. The only thing that keeps me going is knowing I had success in Charleston and New Orleans. Surely I can work hard enough to find the same success here.

Then, after a couple more disappointing weeks, something rather unexpected happens. I'm in my hotel room answering emails when Hal calls. He says, "Look, Viv, I had another tech assignment hit my desk this morning. It'd be a breeze for you. Do you want to swap assignments?"

Hal has never, *not ever*, let me even *consider* swapping out assignments. Tech companies are pretty easy; I can offer more money and my feminine persuasions. It might lead me to that promotion faster. "What do you think? I've never abandoned an assignment before."

Hal pauses a moment before answering. "I have my doubts about this healthcare system in Nashville. We don't have much to work with from a recruitment standpoint and they're not cooperating as much as I'd like. However, you're also the best on my team, so if anyone can make it work, it'd be you."

I'm glad we're on the phone and he can't see my huge smile. Hal is not one to pay compliments other than 'you did good work, Kid.' "I'll stay on. I want the challenge of something new." I hear Alvin's words about the administration being difficult and not wanting change, but I shut them out.

"I agree you should stay, but we do need to make this work," he says gruffly. I want to make this work. As if I have been slacking off since I got here and now it's time to buckle down. It's annoying, I've been working my tail off.

I agree and as I hang up with Hal, Eugene calls. I smile. *I don't need distractions, but he is a fun one.* I answer, "Hey, what's up?"

"Not much. I wanted to confirm our meeting on Friday. Usual time?"

I walk out to my balcony and soak in the sunshine. "Yeah, that should work fine. Anything specific we need to cover in our meeting?"

Eugene pauses a moment; I can hear the keyboard clicking in the background. "Hang on a sec, I'm walking outside."

"Ohhh…sounds serious."

"Haha. Not really, it's more of an excuse for fresh air. Some days the hospital smells get to me. Can we chat about strategies for performance reviews during our meeting?"

I jot a quick note. "Sure, not a problem. Anything else?"

"Nah. How's your day?"

It's nice to have someone ask about my day other than Lily. "Weird, actually."

"Wanna talk about it? I'm about to go to lunch anyway, so I have some time to chat."

Hmm, maybe. "Uh, just work stuff."

He laughs, "Of course it is, Miss Workaholic. I can be your sounding board. You've done the same for me."

I smile into the phone as I remember walking the streets of Charleston doing just that after I offered him the director position. "Hal said I could abandon my contract in Nashville and take on a tech assignment. It's weird because he's never given me an out before. I always stick with an assignment until it's completed."

"Do you want an out?" He asks.

"I don't think so. I thrive on a challenge. We've not been as successful as we hoped in Charleston or New Orleans. Frankly, Nashville is a disaster. Their administration has NOT been easy to work with here. Our retention and recruitment numbers were acceptable, but not great, in

Charleston and New Orleans. Nashville numbers are coming in well below those. I think if I just put some more time in I can improve those numbers. I want to make it work, so I'd like to stay on. Tech assignments aren't as rewarding, but I can make quick progress. They usually have a decent salary budget I can use as an incentive for hiring."

"I'm sure that helps. I bet you have people who aren't interested in coming back unless there's more money."

I laugh. "Yep! Stubborn people like you!"

He laughs, too. "So tech is easy."

I wouldn't say easy. "Right. Well, it's easier, anyway. I like working in healthcare more. Besides, the tech assignments mean occasionally having to whore myself out. I gotta tell ya, I don't miss that. I haven't done that since I moved to healthcare."

He chuckles. "I can't imagine why you wouldn't miss that. Don't you have a no-sex-for-favors-rule?"
"Well yeah, of course. I don't mean *literally* whoring myself out." *Although Aberlin Consulting would not be opposed to that.*

Eugene laughs again. "I think I need some clarification."

"The last tech assignment was brutal. The hours were awful and I'd been working non-stop for almost two months. I wanted to wrap up badly. I was more than ready to leave Chicago. I had one stubborn recruit. If I got him to sign a contract I could finally leave. I went beyond my normal boundaries to recruit him." *Chad Fitzgerald. I wonder if he's still angry with me.*

Eugene interrupts my thoughts, "Don't leave me hanging - I gotta know how this ends!"

"Maybe I ended up sitting on his lap and *strongly indicated* that more was coming as soon as I wrapped up my work at his firm." Ugh, it seems even worse when I say it out loud. *Why am I even admitting to this behavior anyway?*

"Wait."

"What?" I ask, genuinely perplexed. I glance at the time, I should end this call soon. I need to be working.

"Were you wearing your lucky black skirt?" he asks.

What is he getting at? "Yeah. I know it didn't work with you, but it usually does."

Eugene groans and responds with mock indignance. "You weren't sitting on my lap when you were wearing it! I didn't know that was an option. Why didn't I hold out longer?!"

Such a flirt. "I'm so sorry to disappoint you. It was an isolated incident. Not my norm, for sure."

Eugene mumbles something about lucky tech guys and I start laughing, not fully catching his words. He continues, "You're gonna have to make it up to me."

He's so ridiculous. "I am?"

"Yeah, I want that level of consultant. How does that work? Can I put in a request? I'll even do paperwork. You know how I hate paperwork."

I shake my head. *He does hate paperwork.* This conversation's getting out of hand. "Eugene. Anytime I use overly flirtatious behavior it's completely a charade. Like an actor fulfilling their role. It's not real. It's never real."

There's a stretch of brief silence as the tone of the conversation changes from playful to serious. Eugene breaks the silence. "Everything with us has been real. We've never been just a charade, Vivian."

I swallow hard as emotions rise to the surface. *He's not wrong.* My words escape before I can overthink them. "I know."

"Do you want more?"

"More?" I ask, trying to buy myself some time. I don't love where this conversation is heading. It makes me feel uneasy.

He hesitates, for just a moment. "Yes, more."

More? How elusive. I try to keep the tone light and teasing. "Our location difference makes a booty call a bit inconvenient, don't you think?"

Eugene sighs. "That's not what I'm asking for and you know it."

Silence on my end. *How do I even respond to that?*

"Vivian, I'm asking you to be my partner. My girlfriend. Whatever you want to call it. I have no doubt a booty call with you would be epic, don't get me wrong. I want more, though. I need more. We could do long-distance."

I feel like I can't breathe. I go back inside and sit on my bed. I ask for clarification, another stalling tactic. Clarification isn't necessary. He's being perfectly clear. I just don't know what to do with this information. "You're asking if I want to be your *girlfriend*?"

"Yeah. I am. I want to be more than friends. I care about you. I think about you all the time. I want more."

Once again, silence from me. I have a hunch he didn't plan to broach this subject today. Yet, here we are. *Is this really happening?*

He doesn't allow me to escape the question. "Do you want more?"

I start pacing my hotel room again. *That's it. The question that has been unspoken between us all this time is now out in the open. How could I possibly juggle more when I can't even handle my career right now?*

Every part of me is screaming, yes! *I want this Eugene, I want YOU.* Except for my brain. So instead, I mutter, "It doesn't matter what I want. I don't have more to give. My job takes everything. I've gotta go."

I hang up before he can argue further. Or convince me into a relationship I know I don't have the bandwidth to handle.

I close my eyes and take a few deep breaths trying to wrap my brain around what just happened. He sends a simple text. One that helps me solidify my plan.

> If you want this, if you want us, we can make it work. I get how consuming your job is. I wouldn't ask for more than you can give.

Too late. He just asked for more than I can give. I don't reply. Pushing him away doesn't feel right, but it's my only option. If I'm going to be successful in Nashville, then I need to keep a laser-sharp focus on work. If I can manage success in Nashville, maybe it will be enough to finally be promoted.

Then, I can have some kind of life outside work. Maybe. Hal works long hours and weekends too, even if he doesn't travel.

I stay another month in Nashville. Most days I have missed calls or messages from Henrietta and Lily. Every day I hear from Eugene. Sometimes I just say I can't chat, other times I hit ignore, I don't have time for them anymore. I'm drowning in work and have no idea when I'll be able to come up for air. I push away the guilt of knowing I am letting them down.

This is why relationships are hard for me, I just don't have the time to devote to them.

Maybe I can push them away completely, except for Lily. She's too stubborn. She'd say something about a sister's bond cannot be broken. But Henrietta? She's better off without me. Eugene is too, though he doesn't realize it yet. I can't cut them off completely, not yet, since we still work together. Maybe I can keep it strictly professional though. *Work is my life, I can't have more of anything else.*

Escape

Emma, another RN, calls me and is willing to talk. She left the hospital over a year ago, so I'm grasping at straws here. But that's all that's left - I have nothing else.

We meet for coffee and she greets me politely. "Nice to meet you, Vivian. I'm not coming back to the hospital - ever - but I heard you came here and I want you to know why I left."

I start running through guesses in my head. Sexual harassment. Violence. Idiotic managers. Turns out, she's got a brand new reason.

She sits down and begins her story. "I was working on the oncology floor. It's hard work. Cancer is an ugly and unrelenting beast. I'm used to my patients dying. It's sad to say, but you get calloused to it. You have to if you want to be a functional person. But then, there was Fernando."

I nod, allowing her to continue. If I knew what was good for me, I'd leave this conversation right now. It has no potential to lead me to my goals. I'm a glutton for punishment apparently - I stay. I have to know what happened.

"My patient was early 30s. Hispanic male. End-stage cancer, he was dying. Beyond our ability to save him. It didn't have to be; he had treatable cancer initially. He didn't seek treatment initially, being Hispanic. Many Hispanic people typically don't seek medical care for fear of deportation. I'm reading through his chart. As in an official medical document, right? In the documentation, his doctor said that he just needed to go back to Mexico and die. That didn't even rattle me much. Like I said, I've worked in bad situations." She absently folds her napkin, never maintaining eye contact for long.

"That was the doctor's plan written in the chart? To send him to Mexico to die?" *Surely I'm not hearing this right.*

She shrugs. "Yeah, that was the plan. It's cold, but I've heard of worse plans."

I cannot possibly fathom a worse plan, but I just nod for her to continue.

She gathers her thoughts and then continues, "Anyhow, I go in to meet this guy and everything's fine. He's a sweet gentleman. I get him whatever he needs. But then his wife walks in. She has a toddler. Maybe two years old, with big expressive eyes and wearing a superhero shirt. She puts him down and he runs to my patient and crawls in his lap. The cutest kid I've ever seen. And I was crazy to ask the next question. Insane really. I asked my patient if that was his son. He said yes, this is Fernando."

"Fernando is the little boy?" I ask. I know it is, but feel like I need to say something, anything.

She stops fidgeting and looks me dead in the eye. "Yes, Fernando. Who will lose his dad because healthcare didn't feel that his dad was worth saving. Fernando, who will grow up without the love of his father, who won't even remember his father. We decided his father should just go away and die. Fernando may face deportation, poverty, and possibly starvation. Who knows what else? He's got more problems at age two than most of us have in a lifetime."

"He's just a baby…" I shake my head.

"Exactly zero of these problems are his fault. I was in the room and felt like I was suffocating. I excused myself and I ran to the back stairwell. No one uses it. I sat on the cold, hard stairs as my heart shattered. That toddler did me in, Vivian. My heart broke for him and I have not recovered."

The sting of unshed tears burns my eyes. "Emma. That's why healthcare needs you. It needs people who care. People with heart."

She stood up and the sadness in her eyes was replaced by an unmistakable anger. "Until healthcare is for everyone, then it might as well be for no one. I'll have no part of it." She storms away, leaving me behind. I close my eyes and allow a few tears to fall.

Eugene calls me at this exact moment and I answer automatically, before remembering I vowed to push him away. I haven't talked to him in days. The conversation with Emma is still swirling around in my brain and I am not thinking straight.

He exclaims into the phone, "She answers! Are you done avoiding me?"

"Eugene, I can't do this." Suddenly the exhaustion has caught up with me full force. *I could sleep for days.*
"Vivian, please let me apologize. I'm so sorry. I didn't mean to make things weird between us. We can keep our friendship as it is if that's what you want. I care about you. I want to be in your life, in any capacity."

"That's all I can offer right now," I say. I doubt we can just go back to the way things were. Not after he said he wanted more from me. *More than just a hook-up.*

"What's your schedule look like for the next couple of weekends? I'm off work and could fly into Nashville."

"No..." I trail off, trying to figure out how I can avoid seeing Eugene again. Ever. *For his sake.*

"Bad timing? Or do you not want to see me? We can just hang out. No pressure of anything more from me."

Of course I want to see him! Therein lies the problem. I can't keep wishing for something more when this is my life. Hotels. Airports. Over and over again. Nothing permanent. No stability. I don't need friends.

"Sorry Eugene, I'm drowning in Nashville. Nothing is working out. I'm working 60-70 hours a week or more trying to tie up loose ends in New Orleans and Charleston while trying to deal with this trainwreck hospital in Nashville. Hal's furious about my lack of success here. I don't usually make friends for this reason. This is my life. I wouldn't blame you if you don't want to be a part of it," I say, tempting him to take the bait and ditch me. I'm not strong enough to do it.

Full disclosure? I could absolutely take the weekend off and hang out with Eugene. It's not like working extra hours is helping me. I know if I spent any time with him, I'd yank him out of the friend zone at lightning speed. *Where would that leave us? I'm still gone all the time. I'm still not able to even consider a relationship with him.*

Eugene interrupts my thoughts. "Is that why you've been avoiding me lately? Or is it because I said I wanted more?"

I'm so very tired. "You don't need to apologize for saying you want more. I appreciate the honesty."

"But, you don't want more? That's why I haven't heard from you?"

I hate being called out. "Eugene, I'm not worth your trouble. I'm working nonstop, no end in sight. I'm so drained. I don't have anything left to give. I'm a horrible friend."

Eugene sighs. "You're not a horrible friend."

Ugh! Why won't he take the bait? Shut things down between us? I'm not strong enough to do it. His pull on me is too great. "Yes, I am! You don't need me."

"I'm not the kind of person who gives up on a friendship just because schedules are crazy. Give me some credit here, Vivian."

"Eugene..."

He interrupts. "I'm not even upset, although perhaps disappointed. I was gonna buy a crazy large cowboy hat when I was in Nashville. Maybe learn a line dance."

I laugh. I can't help it. It breaks the tension. "Sorry to disappoint you. Maybe they have a cowboy shop in Charleston?"

"No, no, it's not the same. Gotta go to Cowboy Country for the real thing."

I try to think of something else to say, but just try to end the conversation with a lame, "gotta run."

"Vivian, wait..."

I close my eyes and look for peace of mind. *I don't find it.* "Yeah?"

"I understand your life is crazy right now, but I still very much want to be a part of it. Even if you've friend-zoned me."

Oh, Eugene. I didn't mean to hurt you. Hurting you hurts me, too. "I don't know if or when it'll get better."

"I know. If you don't want me to be a part of your life, that's one thing. But if you do want me around, we can make it work."

I sigh. He's sweet, but he's so wrong. "I'm sorry, I gotta go." I can't bring myself to tell Eugene I don't want him around. *I hate myself for it.* I hang up the phone and tears silently fall. I blame it on exhaustion and not on the fact I'm pushing away people who clearly, mysteriously, and stupidly care about me. I quickly brush the tears away, I don't need the people in the coffee shop to think I'm having a breakdown.

Lily texts me later that afternoon and asks when I'll be back in Raleigh. I slam my fists against my desk, suddenly angry. Very angry. Everyone knows I work. Only work. Why do people want more from me? I can't have another life, there are no other options. I text back Lily a single word: "Never." She calls, but I ignore it.

I work until late evening but can't get the conversation with Eugene out of my head. He's willing to come to me and make sacrifices for me. I've offered nothing in return. I desperately want him around. *I can't take the next step with him. I just can't.*

The walls around me feel like they're closing in; my hotel room feels as small as a matchbox. I can't escape my overactive brain. All my deep breathing and relaxation techniques are just not working. I head Downtown for a walk. I stop at a pub and listen to a local band. I meet a guy there and he's very much a willing candidate for Mr. Nashville. Someone who would enjoy the short-term and not require an actual relationship from me. He's in my space and he's whispering sweet nothings in my ear. *Everything is going perfectly - Mr. Nashville is an ideal distraction. A perfect escape.* He takes my hand and we head to the dance floor.

I'm dancing with Mr. Nashville and I don't really dance or even know how. But that doesn't seem to matter much; he pulls me close and I follow his lead. My heart isn't in it, anyway. But I need to find my way back to me - or who I used to be. Except the person I used to be doesn't feel like me either. I fake smile at Mr. Nashville and desperately try to convince myself this is fun.

Everything is fine. *Totally fine.* Then, he points at somebody's cowboy hat. That makes me think of Eugene and I don't want to be here. *I didn't think the emptiness inside could get worse, but it turns out I was wrong.* Awkwardly and abruptly I leave Mr. Nashville. I just shrug and give a lame apology. I pretend to have an important phone call. I go back to my hotel, alone. As I should be. I'm on the brink of calling Eugene back, to promise I'll make time for him. I want him to know that he matters to me. But I'm afraid it's all promises I can't keep. I low-key panic, thinking that I've lost the chance to be with him. *I can't do it, I can't take that step.*

I never make the phone call.

The next day, I can't stop thinking about Eugene. I need *something*, so I call Henrietta. It's a mistake because, at the sound of her voice, I remember how much I miss her, too. I should be pushing her away and I regret I called her. But she's a safer choice than Eugene.

"Girl, I have missed you! Where have you been?!?" Henrietta all but yells into the phone.

"I've missed you, too! Sorry, I've been MIA." I say. And it's true. We catch up on work drama and thrift finds. It's like I'm still there with her in New Orleans.

"Love, Ethan was calling me every day. He even stopped by a couple of times. One day, I had to hide behind my couch while he looked in the window."

I laugh at the mental image. "Sorry to bring this up again, but wouldn't it be easier to talk to him?"

"I did," she says slowly uttering the words.

Say what?! "You did talk to him?"

"I was afraid to. He's irresistible. But yesterday he was waiting for me by my car when I was leaving work. I didn't have a choice in the matter."

Man, Ethan didn't give up, I'll give him that. "What happened?"

"I told him that his proposal threw me. I mean it freaked. me. out." Henrietta sighs.

I prop up on my hotel bed, hugging my knees. "Did he have any explanation why he wanted to marry now?"

"He has a brother, several years older than him. Still, they're pretty close. His brother was diagnosed with pancreatic cancer." Henrietta's voice is strained; I can hear the hurt.

"How awful. What are the treatment options?" *Anything with the word cancer is scary.*

"Pancreatic cancer is a death sentence. The survival rate is extremely low." I can hear the pain in her voice.

"Oh, no. Poor Ethan." I hug my knees tighter. Life can be so cruel.

"Yeah. Ethan is *a mess*. He proposed to me because he realized life is short. He felt like he wasn't moving through life fast enough. I can't do that…" Henrietta trails off.

"Can't do what?" I ask. One of the problems with having friends is that their pain becomes your own. *I wish I could go back to being a robot.*

"I can't be just an item to be checked off life's to-do list. I can't marry because Ethan suddenly realizes life is short. We were never end-game, anyway. I see that now. We broke things off for good."

I have no idea what to say to that. "Ugh. Men."

"Haha! Got that right! How's your boy?"

Amazing. Perfect. A magnetic force that won't let me go. "I don't know. About fed up with me, I think. He told me he wanted more. Not a weekend hook-up, like an *actual* relationship."

"Ohhh… That's an interesting development. I wish we could talk about this while thrift shopping."

I chuckle."Me too. I knew Eugene was attracted to me, sure. But I didn't know he cared for me. What am I supposed to do with that information?"

"You care for him, too? Right?" Henrietta is so direct, always going to the core of an issue.

"Yeah. I've tried not to, but I do. I thought the feeling would fade the longer I was away from Charleston. If anything, it's stronger." My answer is honest. It feels weird saying that out loud. *I do care for him. That's annoying.*

"You choose the next chapter. No one else. Remember that, Love."

She's the best of friends. "Yeah. You too. I'm sorry about Ethan."

"Our break up was inevitable. I don't regret it. Ethan and I had a lot of fun times together."

We chat a little longer before we hang up. While it was so comforting to talk with Henrietta, she's another distraction I don't need right now. For the next three weeks, I bury myself in work. I make excuses when my sister calls.

I avoid Henrietta other than an occasional text to make sure she's doing okay. I completely avoid Eugene - I even cancel our work meetings. *He doesn't take the hint.*

I miss you, milady.

Just let me know if you're okay.

Nothing but silence, is that really how it's going to be?

No matter what I do, I can't seem to achieve the same level of success in Nashville as I did in New Orleans and Charleston. Hospital administration isn't willing to make changes. Nurses don't want to come back, many of them rightfully so. I keep hitting my head against the wall. I have a nagging thought that I was more successful when I had friends and a better work/life balance. I shove that thought down. I start working even more hours, thinking surely I can get some traction if I just try harder.

But the traction never comes and in the meantime, I've ostracized the only people who care about me. Hal thinks we need a new strategy and asks me to prepare a presentation outlining the challenges I've faced.

I'm supposed to fly to New York and give my presentation Friday morning to Hal and the other Lead Consultants. I work on the presentation the rest of the week and fly out early Friday morning.

I've spent hours on my presentation and feel fairly confident in giving it. I freshen up from my flight in the lobby bathroom and ride the elevator up to the conference room. Breathe in, breathe out. I close my eyes and center myself. It helps to calm my nerves. I walk in smiling. I set up my visuals; I only have a few slides. But mostly I plan on talking. Telling stories. Putting faces and experiences behind a bullet-point list of challenges facing healthcare.

I take one more deep breath and start, "It's the one thing we all have needed, need now, or will need in the future. The necessity of healthcare is as sure as death and taxes. But as we all too often see with those in essential personnel, they're not treated well. Society deems healthcare providers as indispensable. However, the indispensability isn't shown in how they're treated by their administration, management, or the patients that they have vowed to serve."

I glance around the room and pause for a moment. I go into how healthcare directors use strict productivity measures and micromanaging. I talk about inflexible bosses and the need for better management training across the board.

Then I talk about how healthcare providers face verbal assault and increasingly more common physical assault. Many face sexual harassment from patients. Oftentimes they miss lunch, miss birthday dinners, miss holiday celebrations, all for patients and administration teams who don't bother to show even a modicum of appreciation. All for a paycheck that's subpar.

I end on a more positive note, showing that change is slow - but it can be done. Improved security. Promoting healthcare providers to management and administrative roles has positive outcomes; they're well-suited for these positions. Proactively working with universities on the recruitment of new graduates minimizes staffing shortages.

I start to close, knowing that being long-winded will not serve me well. "One thing that's important to recognize is that the healthcare field is a high burnout field. Unfortunately, there's no way around that reality. At times these people need to step away and take a sabbatical. Their mental health requires it and administration teams need to be sensitive to that need. Working in life-and-death circumstances will, of course, take a toll on the minds and hearts of these workers. If we want to keep them around - and we certainly do - then we need to allow them the breaks they need to be refreshed and rejuvenated."

I pause here, looking around the room, "Some healthcare practitioners are wounded beyond repair and are unable to return to their field. These people do not need our admonishment, but our gratitude for their service."

I finish my presentation and idly start putting things away while people mingle. A few of the attendees give me polite "thank you" and "nice presentation" comments, though none of it feels very genuine. Just surface-level niceties. I doubt anyone enjoyed my talk, and why should they? While I was able to weave in some optimism, the overall outlook of healthcare is rather bleak. I don't know that our firm can do much about it, other than continuing to provide support for recruiting and building better departments for employee retention. I'm zipping my laptop into my bag when Hal whispers to me, "Meet me in my office."

Fantastic. This should be fun. I rub my temples and try to mentally prepare myself for a meeting with Grumpy Hal. I smile and wave at his assistant, Victoria, as I enter his office. He sits behind his obnoxiously large desk. I take the chair across from him and prepare myself. His jaw is clenched, and he seems a bit more than grumpy, angry, maybe.

Before he's able to say anything, his facial expressions turn from anger into panic. His hand clutches his chest and he collapses to the floor with a resounding thud.

"No, no, no, no, no!! VICTORIA!! CALL 911!!" I run to the opposite side of his desk where he collapsed on the floor. I pull him away from his chair. *He's not breathing.*

Henrietta made me take her CPR class when I was in New Orleans, just a few weeks ago. I hear her echo in my head now, "You never know what life is gonna throw at you, Love. It's best to be prepared." I think I'm supposed to check for a pulse first. Victoria is kneeling beside me, talking to 911.

"No pulse. He's not breathing. I'm going to start chest compressions," I announce, sounding much more confident than I actually am.

Victoria updates the 911 operator. "She's starting chest compressions. It's 10:39 a.m."

Philip from the office next door comes in; I see him out of the side of my eye. "Paramedics are coming - make sure they can find us."

Philip is fortunately calm in a crisis. "On it. There's an AED in the break room - I'm going to grab it."

Victoria continues to update the 911 operator. Fortunately, the paramedics are close. Philip comes in and says "I can take over compressions if you know how to do the AED."

I don't know how to do it at all - I mean I did it on a dummy in the CPR class. But I hear Henrietta's voice in my head again, "Anyone can use an AED. It'll tell you what to do." She's right, the electronic voice talks me through the steps for the setup. The voice tells us to clear and I push Philip away. It delivers a shock and we watch as Hal's body convulses. At that very moment, the paramedics come in. I have never, not ever in my entire life, been so happy to see someone.

As they take over, I start to shake. My knees feel weak as I try to process this unexpected turn of events. *Is Hal going to be okay?* Philip puts an arm around me, "You probably saved his life. You were calm under pressure. I'm impressed."

A paramedic never stops working, but says, "He's right, you know. I'm guessing he had a heart attack. His heart is beating again, thanks to all of you."

They slide him onto a stretcher. Victoria gets the details about where they're taking him.

She comes up to me and asks me if I want a flight home. "No… no, I can't leave. I want to make sure he's okay."

She's scrolling through her phone. "There's a hotel a couple blocks from the hospital. I'm going to get you a room. We use them a good bit. You've probably stayed there before. I'm going to wrap up a few things here and then meet you at the hospital. I'll need to clear Hal's schedule. You may want to check in at the hotel. It'll be a while before they can tell us anything anyway." In a flash, she sent me all the details. I'm grateful because I still don't have a fully functioning brain.

I thank her and make my way to the front lobby. I open the door and head out to the crowded streets of NYC. I'm about to hail a cab but change my mind. I have my laptop and carry-on luggage with me, but I decide to walk anyway so I can clear my head. I'm navigating the busy sidewalk when I get a call from Victoria who tells me Hal is undergoing a heart catheterization and we won't be able to see him for a few hours.

I check into my hotel room and grab a sandwich from the front desk. My stomach is churning but I'm hopeful some food will help it settle. I change into some comfortable clothes. I'm physically exhausted, so I make myself a cup of coffee. My head is spinning too much to rest. I text Henrietta to tell her thank you for making me take the CPR class, and that I had to use those skills today.

Immediately she responds:

Can't chat now but I need DETAILS. SOON.

While I'm reading her text, a reminder pops up on my phone that I have a meeting with Eugene today at 2 p.m. Timing-wise, I can make it. I should make it since I've canceled our last few meetings. I just don't think I can manage it mentally after the events of this morning. I make a mistake and call Eugene instead of just shooting him a quick text.

"Vivian Ashmead. To what do I owe this unexpected pleasure? Are you speaking to me again?" His voice is strained.

I can't deal with that right now, so I ignore it. "Can we reschedule our meeting?"

"Sure, I can reschedule. I assumed you'd cancel it anyway. Again."

"Eugene, it's just..." I can't say anything more. I hear my voice crack. I don't even sound like me.

"Everything alright?" His voice sounds distant.

To my absolute and complete horror, I burst into tears. I am shaking and sobbing uncontrollably. I can't seem to choke out any words.

"Vivian?! What happened?! I'm here, I'm ready to listen when you can talk. I'm not going anywhere. I've got you."

I desperately try to compose myself and manage to choke out, "I had to use an AED today. I did CPR."

"An AED? As in a defibrillator?"

I manage to choke out, "Yes."

"Are you serious?! Of course, you're serious. I imagine you were terrified. I would be."

I've calmed down a little and can explain further. "My boss, Hal, had a heart attack, I think? He collapsed and I did CPR because I couldn't find a pulse. I did a class in New Orleans on how to do CPR. My friend, Henrietta, made me take it. I'm so glad she did. He's having a catheterization right now, I think? I don't even know what that means." The last words come out as strangled sobs. I fall apart again.

Eugene explains a heart catheterization to me. It's calming to hear his voice. I feel some of the tension melt away. *His voice is the one I needed to hear.*

He continues, "I'm proud of you. But, are you okay? That's quite a traumatic ordeal, especially to manage alone. I can come to you if you need support?"

"I'm doing okay, thank you. It's a kind offer." It's a blatant lie. *I am nowhere near okay.* I continue, my words still punctuated with tearful sobs, "Can I call you later? Maybe tomorrow? It does help to hear your voice."

"You can always call me. I wish you would call me."

"Eugene, I … it's just …" I fall apart again, unable to control the onslaught of emotion. *I've missed Eugene desperately.*

"Are you sure you don't need more?"

I definitely need more. "No, I'm okay. I'm so sorry for breaking down."

"I don't care that you broke down, milady." The soothing sound of his words brings me peace.

I continue, "I'm not even sure how long I'll be here or where I will be sent next. We were going to discuss whether or not I should continue in Nashville. Hal being in the hospital changes things, but I don't know how, exactly."

"Keep me posted, yeah? The offer stands if you change your mind."

I promise to keep him updated and we hang up. *Why does he even care? I've done my best to cut him out of my life.* I go to the bathroom to wash my face with cold water. I grab a small bag with my phone charger, some trail mix, and my water bottle. I head out to the hospital. I'm not sure what to expect, but I'm anxious to check on Hal.

Victoria's already in the hospital waiting room, but Hal is feeling groggy and refusing visitors. However, he did make it through the procedure without any complications. The nurse tells us to come in the morning for a visit. I grab some soup from a nearby diner and head back to my room. I eat it and fall asleep the instant I lay down. I'm exhausted from the shock of everything.

The next morning I wake up to no updates from Victoria. Eugene has checked in a couple of times, and so has Henrietta. I send them both a quick text that Hal seems to be doing better and I'm going to check on him.

I'm up early and I make it over to the hospital a little before 8 a.m. I am pleased to see Hal is awake and looking so much better. Relief washes over me. While Hal is talking with Victoria, I call the diner where I got soup last night and pay for them to deliver bagels to the unit's staff. It's the least I can do. *Hal is going to be okay.*

"Viv. I guess I have you to thank for saving me." I sit down next to him and he squeezes my hand. It's the most affection we have ever shared.

"It was a group effort. I'm just so glad I took the CPR class in New Orleans a couple of weeks ago."

Hal asks me for the details of what happened; he has no memory of any of it. He continues, "Really, I might not be here without you, Kid. Viv, I need to level with you. I'm done."

"Done?" I ask.

"I spoke with my cardiologist today. She said that I had too much stress in my life and that it was killing me. I need to retire."

"I'm sorry, what did you say?" Surely I didn't hear him right. His words just don't seem to register.

Hal chuckles. "I know it's hard to believe this old curmudgeon is hanging up his hat. But I need to. I want to enjoy life while I still have some time. I was putting things in place to retire anyway, but my health requires me to speed up the timeline. I'm only going back to Aberlin to clean out my desk."

"Hal..." I start, but I don't know what to say. Retiring? Really?

"I have a meeting set up with you and Philip today. You'll have to leave soon. Look, your presentation on the challenges of these healthcare contracts was not encouraging. But remember, you have an advantage over everyone else - you're the only one with boots-on-the-ground experience with these types of contracts. While Philip and I may not be totally happy with the way things went, you were successful. For the most part."

I nod, still trying to absorb the shock of everything.

"Viv, when you meet with Philip, remember everything I taught you."

"That's your only advice?" How unnecessarily cryptic.

"You'll know what to do, Kid." We say our goodbyes and I head back to Aberlin. I do some deep breathing and try to settle my mind. Hal was grumpy and unreasonable at times, but he has been my mentor. A good mentor, for the most part. It feels odd to be moving on without him. I don't know Philip very well and I have zero time to prepare for this meeting. I'm going to have to wing it. *That's not my strength.*

I enter Philip's office and he gets right to business. He had to work in a meeting with me in between his other commitments today. He talks of how I've been an asset to the company and have a bright future at Aberlin. He gives a broad outline of a new position.

"You're offering me Hal's job?" I ask. *Is this the moment I've been waiting for?!*

Philip leans back in his chair. "Not exactly. It's a step above where you are in both salary and responsibility. However, you would report to me over the next year. The truth is we need someone who is still willing to travel. Hal hasn't traveled for assignments in years. He delegated the bulk of his work to his staff. Hal's strength was finding great people, people like you. We have more healthcare contracts coming in and you're the only one with any experience in that field."

Something feels off. "What would you foresee the next year looking like, schedule-wise?"

"I see that you started in Charleston, then you went to New Orleans, and then Nashville. You were able to keep three assignments going at once. Is that right?"

"Yes, that is correct." I left unsaid that I was drowning in work by the time I got to Nashville.

"I need you to keep doing that. Managing multiple assignments as you move along. I know it's hard work, which is why I'm offering the salary increase. I have a meeting I can't get out of right now, can you meet me back here in an hour so we can discuss moving forward? You can stay in my office. I'd like to finalize your new position today."

I nod in agreement and Philip passes me a folder.

"Salary and benefit specifics are included, as well as a tentative schedule for the next year. I know Hal was not one to plan ahead; he liked to see how things took shape before committing to the next step. I'm not that way; I've got the next year mapped out." He leaves for his meeting and I start reviewing the contents of the job offer.

First impression? This offer is good money. Not Lead Consultant money, obviously, but still a significant bump in salary. The schedule is brutal, with only a few days off at the end of the year. But if I could just stick it out for another year, maybe I could have Hal's job - one that is mostly stationary. A job where I could build a life and have some stability.

I start pacing around the room. Was Hal happy, though? Not really, but was that his natural disposition or because of his career? Hal also said the stress of the job was damaging his health. *Would that eventually happen to me, too?*

I pace some more, my mind unsettled. Can I trust Philip? Would he put me in Hal's position after a year? I've worked for this - worked really hard for it. *I deserve the promotion.*

I sit down for a minute - pacing in heels is hard on my feet. I absently check my phone and see I have a text from Eugene. I take a deep breath and ignore the message. Eugene tends to shatter my focus. I reread the job offer and something feels off. I've written my fair share of job offers. I know something here isn't right even if I can't put my finger on it immediately.

I stand up, too restless to sit, and walk over to the picture window overlooking the busy city streets. Here I am, on the precipice of everything I've ever wanted; everything I've ever worked for is finally within my grasp. In a year, I could be taking Hal's position and having people work for me. Just one more year of hustle and then I could settle down. 365 days more. I could do it.

It's right at an hour when Philip returns. I steel myself to ask the one question that has been plaguing my mind. "Philip, why not promote me to Hal's position now?"

It's somewhat of a bold move - rumor has it people don't often question Philip. He has a larger-than-life persona.

He's surprised by my words. "I thought I was clear on that point, was I not? We need someone who can travel and manage multiple assignments."

"I can hire people to do that. You've promoted me to a level of consultant that doesn't even exist in our company structure. You made a position for me." I've done that too. *I've made positions for people before. It's rarely in their best interest.*

He offers a tight-lipped smile. "Can you hire someone as good as you? You're already trained to do it."

"I could train others to do it, like Hal trained me. I've looked at the schedule and it's not conducive to success. My last assignment in Nashville, as you know, did not go well. Partly because I was still managing two other active assignments." I resist the urge to fidget, instead fighting to at least appear stoic and professional.

"Hal was hard on you about that. Nashville was successful, just not to the same degree. We just need some degree of success in each assignment."

Meaning he wants me to do well enough for Aberlin Consulting to get paid, but necessarily not well enough to create meaningful change in my assignments.

The quality of our work is not the focus, the bottom line is the focus. It's reminiscent of Eugene talking about healthcare. "These are still healthcare contracts? For the next year? I'd need to continue the same work for another year before Hal's position is in reach?"

He shrugs noncommittally. "That's the ballpark goal, sure."

"You're not going to rehire his position before then?" I ask. *I already know the answer.*

"Of course not. It's yours in the next year or so."

I grit my teeth. "Philip, I know that game. You'll wait until I'm busy on another assignment and hire Hal's position behind my back. I've done it myself. Hal taught me how to do it."

He snorts. "What choice do you have? I'm not Hal. I am not you either. Your only choice is to trust me."

Except I don't trust him. Warning bells and red flags are everywhere. I don't have to agree to anything he's offering. I do have a choice. *Henrietta was right! I CAN write the next chapter.* The shock of my next move will reverberate through my entire being for days. I stand up and gather my things. I unceremoniously toss my badge on his desk. "You'll have an official resignation letter by the end of the day. I'm done."

Philip slowly stands up. He towers over me - he towers over almost everyone. He's well over six feet tall. "Don't do this, Vivian. You're a smart girl. Did you not see the salary? You won't clear half of that anywhere else."

I am a smart girl. *Smart woman. Smart enough to see smoke and mirrors in play.* I saw the bump in pay. While it's good money, it's not nearly what I would make in Hal's position. I also saw my entire life continuing to be consumed by work. I'm good on the ground. Philip won't promote me; he needs me in the trenches. On some level, I know everything I worked for is starting to unravel. *But I've had enough. No more. It's my choice.* I turn around and smile at Philip. He's red-faced and his hands are clenched. I wave goodbye and keep walking as he yells my name.

It all plays out beautifully. I have my head held high, walking down the hallway. People are coming out of their offices. Philip's behavior has stirred up quite a commotion.

He's infuriated, but I keep my cool as I skip the elevator and take the stairs down to the ground floor. I walk out into the busy city streets and to my hotel. I try some of my deep breathing exercises. I try journaling. I can't do it, my mind is racing too quickly. I feel jittery and unable to settle.

When nothing else calms me, I go for a run. It's exactly what I need. I change my clothes and step into my sneakers. Adrenaline is pushing me forward, clouding me from the reality of my situation. But as my feet once again hit the pavement in Central Park, my euphoria dissipates. I am forced to confront the very real emotion bubbling to the surface. Betrayal. Betrayal with a massive side of panic. *What have I done?!*

I am unemployed, effective immediately. *I'm usually so practical! Why did I jump out of the plane without a parachute? What has gotten into me?! I always have a backup plan.* My running pace picks up a bit. A cold rain begins to fall.

My chest heaves as my lungs try to gulp in desperately needed oxygen. My legs quiver from fatigue. Whenever life is just too much, whenever I need to escape, whenever my other coping mechanisms are a poor substitute, I run.

I run from the echo of my math teacher telling me I'm smart, but not quite smart enough to amount to much of anything.

I run from the embarrassment of eating alone in a high school cafeteria.

I run from the loneliness of never having friends.

I run from the pain of being the awkward and shy kid that others made fun of.

I run when I don't feel strong enough.

I run when depression clouds my soul.

I run to break free. I put literal pavement between me and the monsters I'm facing.

Today I run to escape the betrayal. I've worked so hard, for years, to gain a promotion that would offer me stability only for it to be snatched away. All the long hours and all the hard work evaporate like a wisp of smoke being blown away. Aberlin dangled the promotion in front of me, but would I have ever gotten it? Even if Hal had stayed? I'm not so sure anymore.

I've put in long hours, destroyed relationships, and damaged my health. For what? A company that continually took advantage of me. I don't know what else to do but run. It's the only thing that even makes sense.

Usually running offers me peace and clarity. This time it's different though.

I cannot seem to run far enough or hard enough to escape the betrayal.

The cold air burns my lungs and anger still courses through my veins. I stop and rest my hands on my knees, trying to get my breathing and heart rate under control. I am physically exhausted but my mind is still racing.

I can't run to escape this time. It's simply not working. I have no choice, I'm going to have to face things head-on.

I have a flight home in a few hours. *Home.* I desperately want to leave New York, but I don't want to go home. My apartment doesn't even feel like home, I'm so rarely there. Besides, being at home is going to make it hard to ignore the fact I am unemployed. But home it is, I don't have anywhere else to go. I need to start thinking practically.

I don't want to fly home in wet clothes. I stop by my hotel and grab my things. I peel off my wet clothes and change into leggings and a sweatshirt.

I'm relieved to see my flight is on time. I go to my seat and put in my earbuds. Nothing is playing in them; I just have them in to avoid talking with an overly friendly stranger. I pull out my journal because clearly running did not help me stabilize mentally. I don't write anything down. I just look at the blank pages as they stare back at me.

I'm about to turn my phone off for take-off when I see another text from Eugene.

> Maybe you're embarrassed about crying when we last spoke? I don't care. You're so strong. You don't have to be strong with me. Please let me know how you're doing.

I don't know how to respond. I type a quick text to tell him I need to figure some things out and will contact him later. He deserves that much. For a brief moment, I wonder if my being out of a job changes things between us. I doubt it, *I've probably burned that bridge.* My head is too muddled with other thoughts to sort it out any further.

Hastily, I text Lily before take-off and ask her if she can pick me up from the airport. She asks how long I plan on staying. I don't answer. I just turn off my phone, close my eyes, and listen to the hum of the engine.

Once I've landed and grabbed my luggage, I head outside where Lily is waiting. My sister gets out of the car and hugs me. As soon as I feel her warm embrace, I start tearing up. She looks at me, hugs me again, and whispers, "Whatever happened we can fix it. Together."

"Just take me home, yeah?" As she drives I look out the window, tears still rolling down my cheeks. *I've never been so out of control with my emotions as I have been the last 48 hours, but here we are.* I try to tell her what happened a hundred times on the drive, but I don't even know where to start. So all she gets is unintelligible sentences and choked sobs.

She comes inside with me and lays me on the couch with my favorite blanket. I nap for an hour, I think. I wake up to the smell of potato soup, one of my favorites. I'm groggy but get up. "You cooked for me?"

She smiles. "I remembered you liked it. It's the perfect comfort food."

"Yeah. Thanks, Sis." She spoons me a bowl. I'm famished, but between bites, I relay everything. About the mediocre presentation. About doing CPR. About crying to Eugene. About walking out on my job.

Lily's astonishment is unmistakable. *It's not often I surprise her.* "I can't believe you did that!"

I just bury my head in my hands.

"I do think it might be for the better." She squeezes my shoulder.

Somewhere deep inside I have a hunch that she's right. But it's deep inside. Way, way deep. My entire identity has been entangled in my career for so long. I don't know how to dislodge it. I admit, "I don't even know who I am without work. I have no idea what to do. I just knew I couldn't take the job Philip offered."

Lily puts dishes in the sink and turns to face me. "You're Vivian Ashmead. You've put corporate giants in their place and you've been a friend to a nurse processing trauma. You brought your boss back from the brink of death. You're my sister. You're my hero. There's absolutely nothing you can't do. I have always, *always* been in awe of you."

I meet her gaze and see the sincerity in her eyes. She continues, "But now, you get to do whatever you want, and you get to do it on your terms."

I get to write the next chapter. I give her a fierce hug. No one has a better sister than I do. Her confidence in me gives me strength.

"I can take a couple of months off. I have some savings. I can take off more if I'm frugal."

After I assure Lily that I'm fine and not on the verge of a complete breakdown, she heads home. My apartment just seems so empty. It's never felt like home to me, just a stopping place between work assignments. I never put much thought into what might happen if my career went away. Never considered what I would be left with if my job was gone.

Nothing. I'm left with nothing.

I clean my apartment before going to bed. Surprisingly, I have the most peaceful sleep. I wake up refreshed and ready to face the next challenge. The problem is, I don't know what that challenge is, other than finding a job. But I'm not quite ready to do that. I'm not sure I know what I want to do.

The next day is the same. So is the next. I wake up with no real purpose, no real plan. I reorganize my nearly empty pantry. I clean out closets. I cook. I exercise. I walk to clear my head. I try to journal but nothing comes to me.

Hal calls and I tell him about my meeting with Philip.

"Beautifully executed, Viv."

I roll my eyes. "You think so? Because I'm out of a job now."

"Philip would've never given you my spot. He'd already planned to give it to one of his golfing buddies from another firm. I didn't know that until yesterday or I would have told you. Turns out, I didn't need to. You saw right through him."

I knew I couldn't trust Philip. The pain of the betrayal sinks even deeper. "Smoke and mirrors, you taught me well."

"I asked too much of you, I think. It took me 64 years to realize life's more than just my career. I hope you learn that sooner than I did. You probably will, you're much smarter than I am. I'm a stubborn old curmudgeon." He laughs, he sounds happy. Hal being happy low-key weirds me out.

"I think I do need more than just my career, but I also need a paycheck."

"I'm happy to help you in your job search if you need it."

"I appreciate that. I admit I'm at a loss. I don't know what I want to do." I rub my temples. *I need to get a plan together. Soon.*

"You'll find your path, Kid."

Over the next few days, I start sleeping more and more and after a few days, I'm barely getting out of bed. I don't know how to face life anymore, so I just stay in bed. *It's cozy.*

After a week of wallowing in self-pity, Lily comes over and she just lets herself in since I won't answer the door. *Sisters are infuriatingly stubborn.*

"Vivian, get up and take a shower. I have an appointment for you with my therapist." She yanks the covers off my bed. I'm too drained to argue. I reluctantly take a much-needed shower. I throw on jeans and a tee and pull my hair back into a low ponytail. A glance in the mirror reflects an image I don't recognize.

I break the silence after a few minutes of driving. My tone conveys my annoyance. "Why are you doing this?"

Lily glances over to me and then turns her focus back to the road. "I thought you were doing okay at first. But, you're not. You're spiraling. I only know that because I've gone into a depression spiral before. I know how to recognize it."

"I'm not spiraling," I grumble.

"Yes, you are. You know it, too, or you would've put up a fight for me to get you this far." She reaches over and pats my leg. I don't say anything else. *She's not wrong.*

After the required paperwork, my name is called and I walk into the therapist's office. No sense in denying the obvious: I need help. My shoulders slump and I rest my head on my hand. *Being awake is so hard. I miss my bed.* Without any preamble, I admit, "I'm a mess."

The therapist smiles reassuringly. "At times, aren't we all? Tell me everything."

Over a couple of visits, I relay everything that has happened - from leaving my robotics assignment in Chicago to leaving Philip's office with my head held high but my heart sinking fast.

"My friend, Henrietta, tells me I can start a new chapter, but I feel so stuck. I don't know if I can. How do I move forward?"

I don't like depending on others but my therapist has been Heaven-sent. *If for no other reason, my appointments with her force me out of bed.*

She looks at me thoughtfully. "I have a hunch you're stuck because you have unfinished business in this chapter of your life. It's preventing you from starting the next chapter."

I meet her eyes but don't say anything.

She gives me a knowing grin. She's gotten to the core of my spiral. "Do you have any loose ends you need to tie up?"

Yeah. I think I do.

"Fitzgerald here."

I'm relieved he answered my call. My words have a forced enthusiasm. "Chad! It's Vivian Ashmead."

"I know. I recognize your voice. It's usually laced with lies and empty promises."

Ouch. "That's fair. I'm calling to apologize."

He seems distracted. I did intrude in the middle of the work day. "Look, I don't have time for this right now. I know you were doing your job. I shouldn't have gotten attached."

I pace around my apartment as I talk. My therapist recommended facing things with brutal honesty. Here it goes. "No, this is on me. I definitely led you on. I'm sorry for that. It's wrong to manipulate anyone. Even if you're just trying to escape the bitter cold winds of Chicago."

He chuckles. "I remember you saying you hate Chicago weather."

I laugh, too. "That part was true! So very true. Unlike some of the other things I told you."

"Really, Vivian, it's alright. I don't condone what you did, but I also realize you were probably under a lot of pressure."

He's so much more understanding than I'd be. He's a good guy. "I was under pressure but that's no excuse. I'm sorry. I really am."

He sighs. "It's in the past. I want to escape Chicago myself after my contract is up. I'm looking at a couple of places in Silicon Valley. I hate the weather here, too."

I hesitate. I can make this right, but it's not going to be easy. *Brutal honesty.* "Chad, your contract was for two years."

His tone is suddenly serious. "No, we agreed on just a year."

"I know we did. I wrote it up as a two-year contract anyway." I chew on my lower lip.

He curses under his breath. "VIVIAN!!"

I hold the phone away from my ear. "Wait. Wait. I can make it up to you. I can make this right."

He groans. "Why exactly would I trust you?"

"I understand your hesitation, I do. Just hear me out. I wrote a loophole in your contract. It's going to take some finagling but I can get you out of it, if that's what you want. I always write an escape clause." My words come out quickly. I'm afraid if Chad hangs up on me, he won't take future calls.

He doesn't say anything. I picture him pressing his fingertips to his forehead, his telltale sign of being stressed.

"Can you pull up your contract? Page seven?" I walk over to my laptop so I make sure I have the correct information.

Chad groans again, "Yeah, I guess."

'Look, I understand you don't trust me. I understand why. If I was in your shoes I wouldn't trust me either. But I can make this right, Chad. I owe you that much."

"Isn't this going to get you in trouble with Aberlin?"

Why would he even care if it causes me trouble? I start pacing again. They may try to bill me for the bonus I got securing Chad for two years. Well, they can have the money if it comes to that. "I don't work for them anymore. They screwed me over like I did to you." The words sting when I say them out loud.

He's quiet for a moment. I wonder if he's still on the line. He finally replies "Are you helping me out of spite?"

Brutal honesty. I start talking fast. "Partly, yes. They'll lose money if I weasel you out of a two-year contract. You're amazing at your job, Chad. People fight for you. They fight dirty to get you. I fought dirty for you. You're worth gold. Your current employer doesn't pay you what you're worth. I did tell them that when I was in Chicago. I did advocate for them to increase your salary. I regret that I was unsuccessful. While some of me helping you is spiteful, sure, most of it is that I want to see you in a better place."

He must be able to discern the sincerity in my voice because he agrees. I walk him through the details. It's not easy to terminate his contract, but it can be done. Deep in the fine print, there is a clause that he can take an unpaid sabbatical for up to a year. It takes some complicated paperwork, but I can help with that part.

"Vivian, thank you. You didn't have to do this. It's my fault for not reading carefully in the first place."

"I was purposely pushing you along quickly, hoping you wouldn't notice. That's on me. I'm done with that now. I don't want to be that kind of person." Aberlin turned me into something I'm not. I've been so focused on climbing the corporate ladder that I didn't care about who I stepped on to get there.

We say our goodbyes and I'm about to hang up when Chad says, "Vivian, wait. I don't know how to negotiate for a new job. Do you have any advice?"

Chad's brilliant in robotics, but not so much in negotiations. He needs help to get a salary that reflects his abilities. "I'll help you. Send me your offers and I'll read them over."

"Why would you do that for me? I'm just looking for a couple of tips."

Because I need to right some wrongs. I need to close out this chapter of my life right, on my terms. I need to remember I'm a consultant, not a monster.

"I have no ulterior motives, I promise. Look, I may not have been romantically interested in you. That was all just a means to an end. Again, I'm so very sorry about that. However, I do admire you. In different circumstances, I think we might have been friends. You deserve better than you've been treated. Please, let me help you."

Chad hedges, but then says, "Eh, I do have a couple of offers already."

I smile. I'm not surprised he has offers on the table. He sends them to me. Both are absolute garbage. I send him a checklist of what he needs to ask for and an appropriate salary range for his skills. Both companies are lowballing him. I work an entire day on preparing Chad to demand his worth. It feels kind of like atonement. I can't change the past, but I vow to do better, moving forward.

The next morning I drag myself out of bed. It's hard but manageable. The next day it gets a little easier. So does the next. Lily and I have lunch together. I call Henrietta to apologize for ignoring her calls. I continue seeing my therapist. I'm crawling out of the hole I've been in. I still have one area where I need atonement. One last thing I need to do to close out this chapter of my life.

I wake up one morning and I just cannot see my apartment anymore. Inexplicably, I drive to Charleston. I tell myself I want to feel the cool breeze blowing in from the harbor. Eat at my favorite waterfront deli. It's the first place I go. I finish my lunch and walk around Downtown for a couple of hours. Visit the market and a few shops. The walk clears my head and I have to face the real reason why I'm here.

Eugene.

I've made other friends. But the longing is still there. As I walk I hear his voice echo in my mind.

I'm going to miss you, Vivian Ashmead…

I want to be in your life…

I really want to see you…

If you want more, we can make it work…

I'm sure after dropping him with zero explanation I've burned anything between us to the ground. Regardless, I need to see him so I can find some sort of closure. I text him to let him know I'm in town - simply because it will force me to see him and not chicken out. I feel my heart rate tick up with the thought of seeing him. I've not been fair to him. Shame circles through my mind, unchecked, and I feel a little nauseated.

I need to apologize to Eugene if nothing else. I pulled him away from a job he enjoyed, and for what? I encouraged him to follow the money, only for me to leave money on the table and walk away to nothing. I have exactly zero dollars coming in.

He texts me back after a few minutes.

> It's Halloween next week. I guess the ghosts are coming out.

I roll my eyes. *Funny.*

> Eugene, things have been crazy.

The reply doesn't feel like it aligns with my commitment to brutal honesty. I've been lying in my bed for hours on end, which is not exactly *crazy*. I wait just a few minutes before I feel the vibration of a response.

> Did we ever set a time for our meeting?

It's Friday! Has it been a month since Hal had a heart attack?! We have a work meeting scheduled today. I totally forgot. *I never forget things, ever.* But we don't have a meeting because I don't work there anymore. Ugh!! I'm going to have to tell him that I'm an unemployed loser. Later.

I answer:

> Can we reschedule the work meeting? I do have something I need to discuss, preferably in person. Non-work related.

I chew on my lower lip waiting for a response. It's several minutes before I get one.

> I don't know, Vivian. I'd assumed you were out of my life for good this time.

Fair, I guess. I need to talk to him. I wrack my brain to figure out how to get him to talk to me, short of begging. *Maybe I should beg? I'm not above doing it.* Instead, I keep things simple.

Please let me explain. If you don't ever want to see me after today, I understand.

I'm totally not a basket case waiting for his response, which doesn't come for another half hour. He simply texts me he'll be home around 6:30 p.m. and we make plans to meet at his condo then. I've got a few hours to kill, so I book a hotel for a couple of nights. Fortunately, I have a zillion reward points so it doesn't cost me anything. Sometime soon, I'm going to have to seriously limit my spending. Or find gainful employment.

I freshen up and put on jeans and a floral top I found while consignment shopping with Henrietta. I get in the car and rehearse my apology on my way over to Eugene's. Even in my head, it sounds insincere. I can't seem to find the right words.

He pulls up at the same time I do, so I can't mentally rewrite what I want to say, nor do I have sufficient time to panic.

He's dressed in an untucked, button-down green shirt and khakis. He's as gorgeous as ever, maybe even more so, but he wears an expression of unmistakable hurt. *I probably caused that pain. Fantastic.* He greets me with a hug that lingers, filled with a plethora of unidentifiable emotions. Then he invites me inside.

His condo is clean. Sparse. A few family pictures but nothing more. He has an adorable gray kitten who greets me at the door. She purrs and rubs against my legs. I bend down to pet her.

"Her name is Smokey. My friend's cat had kittens and now I have a kitten." He puts out food for Smokey and she's no longer interested in me.

"I'm sorry." I blurt it out abruptly with no explanation. My rehearsed apology goes out the window. I clear my throat and try again. "I'm sorry I made you quit your chart auditor job where you were happy. I was selfish. I was under a lot of pressure. I was wrong, though. Wrong to do it."

He looks over at me. "You didn't make me do anything. You weren't even that pushy. You already know I didn't love chart auditing. It was … how did you put it? Atrociously boring?"

I smile back at him. "I still need to apologize."
"That's why you came to Charleston? To apologize?"

I shrug. "That and shrimp and grits."

"You're not here to apologize for anything else? For any other reason?"

"What do you mean?" I say evasively as I walk further inside, avoiding eye contact. My mind swirls with thoughts of shame from being unemployed and fear that I've lost the chance to have Eugene in my life.

"Are you serious?" His voice is strained but raises. "I've barely heard from you for weeks."

I didn't think of it from Eugene's perspective when I was wallowing in self-pity the past few weeks. *He has a point.* The silence between us is awkward; I finally break it with a lame apology. "I need to apologize for that, too."

"Yeah, ya think?" His eyes meet mine and I see a mixture of pain and anger.

"I was avoiding you." *Brutal honesty.* What do I have to lose?

"I'm not stupid, Vivian. You've been creating distance between us since you've been in Nashville. Since I asked you if you wanted more." I see a subtle movement of Eugene clenching his fists while he speaks. He's naturally an easygoing guy but my silence over the past few weeks has pushed him to anger.

I hate that I've let you down. "I told you I'm a bad friend."

"Look, I don't care that you're busy. I don't even mind being put on the back burner from time to time. But I need you to be straight with me. Do you want me in your life or not? I can't keep doing this." He gestures wildly between us.

I start feeling a bit defensive, though I have no right to. Eugene is being completely reasonable. "Of course I do, Eugene. I'm here now, aren't I?"

He turns around to face me. "Then why have you been avoiding me? Ghosting me? Then randomly showing up in Charleston? You could've apologized over the phone."

I shrug. "I know."

Eugene's voice is tinted with anger. I realize he wants an explanation, he deserves one, but I can't excuse my behavior. "So why are you *really* here? You've turned me down every single time I've tried to see you, for months now. Rejected my phone calls. Left my texts unanswered. Then you show up in Charleston, completely out of the blue."

"Eugene, that's a loaded question. I'm not sure where to even start…I didn't even know I was coming here before this morning. I just knew I couldn't move on with my life until I came to see you." What else am I supposed to even say? That he is…has always been…a magnetic force that draws me in? That the longing I felt for him in Charleston didn't go away? I'm not entirely sure I even know why I'm here, other than seeking closure. *I can write the next chapter, but I need to make sure this one is finished.*

Eugene's response is only silence. I continue, "I was too embarrassed. I'm still embarrassed. Humiliated, really. I've been trying to sort through things. I don't even know who I am anymore. I was a mess, I was…I am, really…" My voice trails off. I don't know where to start. *Brutal honesty.* I've always felt things with Eugene are complicated, but that doesn't check out. It's quite simple. I do want more. *I've always wanted more.*

I chose my work over any kind of relationship with him. After the intense soul-searching of the past weeks, I realize how I let my career take too much from me. I'm still drowning in anger and shame. I need to recommit to my goal. Today's about closure. If not for my sake, then at least for Eugene's. I imagine he needs a new chapter too.

Eugene still doesn't say anything, he's probably trying to process my incoherent rambling. I go and sit on the barstool in his kitchen. I feel weak. My shoulders slump and I hide my face in my hands. I'm so very overwhelmed by everything and it feels like I'm still drowning. I wonder for the millionth time how I even got here.

"Vivian, what's going on? Please talk to me honestly." He sits down on the barstool next to me and waits.

I take a deep breath in an attempt to calm my racing heart. "Hal retired abruptly. He never went back to work after being in the hospital. He said the stress of work was killing him. He set up a meeting with his associate, Philip, about me staying on at Aberlin Consulting. Philip wanted me to stay, to continue with the healthcare contracts."

"What does that mean?" Eugene tilts his head.

"It means I should've been offered Hal's job!" I slam my hands against the countertop.

He jumps a bit, startled by my toddler-like outburst. "I'm guessing you weren't?"

"Philip made a new position for me, a pseudo promotion. A position between where I was and Lead Consultant - Hal's job. He told me he couldn't promote me to Lead Consultant yet. He needed me to keep traveling and finish our healthcare contracts."

He looks at me until I make eye contact. "I'm not following."

Why does he have to sit so close to me? It's unnerving. I shake those thoughts and continue with my brutal honesty quest. *I wonder what my therapist would think if she were a fly on the wall.* "I walked out on my job, Eugene."

He has the audacity to laugh.

"It's not funny!" I half-heartedly push him away.

He smirks. "Miss Workaholic walking out on her job is a little funny..."

I glare at him, but he just smiles widely at me and I can't be angry. "I did walk out. In the moment it was kind of awesome. Philip was so angry with me! He was screaming at me as I left and I never even looked back. I knew Philip was never going to promote me to Lead Consultant, I *know* that game. I'd be spending at least another year of traveling and long hours. And for what?"

Eugene looks at me intently. "I don't understand. Is that why you've been avoiding me? I don't care if you left your job. Or are you avoiding me because I asked for more?"

My voice is rising and I don't mean it to. But the floodgates of emotion have opened and there's no holding back. "You don't care?! Why would you not care?! I'm an unemployed, hot mess. I worked harder and then harder to prove I was good at my job. Increased my hours every week. All for nothing. I pushed you and everyone else I care about away to try to save my career. I deserved that promotion - I *earned* it. I put all my eggs in that one basket. Now I have nothing."

Eugene gives me a lopsided grin. "So…you do care about me, then?"

Even now, such a flirt. "Is that your takeaway from my rant?" I don't deny it, though. Of course I care.
I care enough to make my next words feel impossibly hard. It's time for a real apology, not just a lame, 'I'm sorry.'"

Eugene sighs deeply. He reaches over and squeezes my hand. The air around us is filled with the whispers of words we've both left unsaid. I feel the comforting warmth of his hand on mine and squeeze back. Here it goes, *brutal honesty. It's time to find closure.*

I turn so I'm facing him. I take both his hands in mine and force myself to maintain eye contact. "I want to clear the air. I chose my career over maintaining some kind of relationship with you, friendship or otherwise. It's not just you; I've been avoiding my sister and my friend, Henrietta, too."

I pause and breathe deeply. *I can do this.* "I've been pushing people in my life away, people who care about me. I thought if I was good at my job, if I could get that promotion, everything else in my life would magically fall into place. I see the naivety of that thought now. I have a mental health therapist helping me sort through some of my faulty thinking patterns. I needed help. I spent days in my bed, refusing to talk to anyone and wallowing in self-pity. I'm a mess now, sure. But I'm so much better than I was a couple of weeks ago."

"Vivian…" His voice thick with emotion. He never finishes his thought. He just squeezes my hand.

I swallow the lump in my throat and force myself to continue. "However, I've treated you the most unfairly. I know I've burned the bridge between us. I regret it deeply, and probably always will. Despite my more recent actions, I want you to know how much you've meant to me. I'll always remember the time we spent together fondly. I'm sorry. So very sorry."

I'm hoping my apology can bring us both some kind of closure. *It feels rather strange to grieve what might have been.*

Eugene paces around the room. I try to say something but he cuts me off. "Vivian, I need a moment. This is a lot to process."

"I can come back tomorrow? Would that be better?"

He hesitates. "No, please stay." Eugene rummages around his fridge. "Do you want something to drink? Eat?"

I just shake my head no.

"Look, Vivian, I admit I'm hurt. Angry. Betrayed. You ghosted me and *that hurts*. The bridge between us is certainly on fire, but it's not burned away. Not completely."

"I would never ask for you to let me back into your life. I just wanted to find some kind of closure. For both of us." I blink away tears that start forming in my eyes. "I'm so sorry, Eugene. I pushed you away because I thought you'd be better off without me."

"I don't need your protection. I just need your honesty. And for you to not drop off the face of the planet for weeks at a time. Maybe I'm crazy for saying this, but I still want you in my life." Eugene sits down next to me and starts gently rubbing my back. My body craves his affection and I lean into his touch.

I take a deep breath and try to settle my emotions. *He wants me in his life? Do we have a shot at staying friends?* "Yeah, I get that now. I do."

"I hate you didn't reach out to me for help." The anger in his eyes has dissipated. *He understands. He gets me. On some level, I always knew he would. Maybe that's what I was most afraid of facing.*

I shake my head. "I couldn't reach out for help after the way I treated you."

Eugene considers this a moment before changing the subject. "Why did this Philip guy not promote you? Do you know?"

I'm still so angry at Philip it hurts - it causes me actual, visceral pain. "Hal found out a couple of days ago that Philip was planning on giving one of his golfing buddies the Lead

Consultant position all along. But having me do all the work, of course."

Eugene flinches. "Wow. Ouch."

Tears fill my eyes again. "Yeah, ouch. I couldn't settle for that. I feel so betrayed."

Eugene pulls me to him and I lay my head on his shoulder. Unable to bottle up my emotions anymore, my silent tears run down my cheeks. He absently runs his hands through my hair. "Of course you feel betrayed! Does he not know how incredible you are? What you've done for our hospital has been amazing. They've implemented new security measures. Helen's working on recruiting and she's a natural at it. We haven't lost any nursing staff in a month. We've only lost one person from the rehab department."

"Really? Who?" I look up at Eugene and jump at the chance of a change in subject. I don't like talking about the current dumpster fire of my life.

He grins sheepishly. "Me. I turned in my resignation today. I was going to call you or tell you today during our meeting. I tried management for several months, but it's not for me. I'm grateful for the opportunity though. You have nothing to apologize for - nothing at all. The extra money from the promotion gave me a financial cushion so I can think about my next step."

"Why didn't you tell me you were unhappy?" Maybe I did make things worse for him, both personally and professionally. *Fantastic.*

Eugene shrugs. "I should have told you. Not that you've given me the chance to tell you anything."

I wince. No point in arguing. *He's not wrong.*

He continues, "I guess I'm not sure I would've told you, even if we had been on speaking terms. Although, I do prefer to be more transparent. I've been trying to sort through some things. Would we still be friends if the job connection disappeared? I wasn't sure. Do you want full transparency? Here it is. I already felt you slipping away and I didn't want to lose the work connection, too. I was worried about losing you completely."

I cannot begin to fathom why he would be worried about losing a workaholic, pathetic excuse for a friend.

I ignore all of that for now and stick to career choices. It seems safer. "You don't have any other work lined up?" I ask.

"Nothing concrete. You?"

"No. Nothing at all." I let out a self-deprecating chuckle and shake my head. I'm unemployed. Unbelievable. *What does the next chapter even look like?*

Eugene smiles. "What does Miss Workaholic do when she's not working?"

I just shrug. *Overthink every day about everything all the time.*

Eugene stands up and starts pacing again. He runs his hands through his hair. It's sticking up everywhere now, which is adorable.

"I could open a clinic here in town - remember the gym wanted an on-site PT? The owners offered to rent me space. It's a good deal. I haven't signed a lease yet. I'm thinking about it for a few more days."

He pauses a moment and then starts pacing again. "I could do travel physical therapy. I've already been talking with a recruiter. I could go anywhere. Live anywhere in the U.S."

"Where would you want to go?"

He stops pacing and turns to face me. "It would be helpful for you to figure out your next move so I know mine."

"What? Why?"

He just looks at me for what feels like an eternity. "Isn't it obvious, milady?"

It's not at all obvious. It's not even in the ballpark of obvious. Does he still want more? Even after all this time? Surely that's not what he means. He closes the distance between us, he's just a breath away. He brushes my hair back from my face with a gentle caress.

He repeats his question in a gentle whisper: "Isn't it obvious?"

I shake my head no and swallow the lump in my throat. With Eugene this close to me I can't seem to speak.

His hands cup my face and he kisses me. Tentatively. Tenderly. Briefly. Much too soon he pulls away and rests his forehead on mine. He lets out a shaky breath. "Vivian, I want to be where you are." He puts his hand around my waist, pulling me off the barstool. His grip is firm enough to invite me into his arms, but not so firm to keep me there. He's giving me the choice. The next move is mine.

I gather my courage and look up into his brown eyes. It feels like an epic moment though I'd never admit it to my sister. If I say yes to Eugene, I'm saying yes to a whole lot more. *I want more. Wanting more in life feels so foreign. Even so, it feels like the beginning of the next chapter.*

I am Vivian Ashmead. I may be an unemployed hot mess, but I refuse to be a coward. I find my voice. "I want to be where you are. I want that, too. We can figure it out." He smiles back at me and it's the most beautiful thing I've ever seen.

He leans in to kiss me again and I blurt out "Wait! Wait. What about James?"

"James?" He's taken aback; who wouldn't be? I don't know when I started blurting out things randomly. He doesn't let go of me, but I do feel him tense up a bit.

"Yes, from HR. James."

A look of confusion crosses his face. "If you're thinking about that crotchety old man right now, I am way off my game."

I smile reassuringly. "No, of course not. Besides, I'm sure you get plenty of practice."

He shakes his head. "No, no one. Not since I met you in that coffee shop. There's been no one else."

"No?" It comes out as a strained whisper.

He brushes my hair away from my face. "No. You created a void in me that nothing could fulfill. I was gutted the day you left Charleston. Hated myself for not telling you how I felt before you left."

"I understand that kind of longing. You were the magnetic force that kept pulling me in, even when I tried to resist it. Even when I tried to push you away. A force that pulled me back to Charleston today."

"Yeah?" He gives me a shy smile.

"Yes."

"Then why are you thinking about James right now?"

I smile, how can I not? "Isn't he retiring soon? We could both stay here, in Charleston. If that's what you want."

Eugene speaks slowly as if his mind is trying to catch up. "He's retiring in a couple of months. Do you want to be the

HR Director? They'd hire you in a heartbeat. You want to stay here?"

I'm still wrapped loosely in his arms. *I could get used to this.* "Only if you do."

"I would love to stay here, but I would also follow you anywhere. I love Charleston. I do. But not as much as I…as I…" He hesitates for just a moment, his eyes searching mine. "Not as much as I love you, Vivian."

"You love me?" My head is spinning with his revelation. *Is this actually happening?*

Eugene leans in and kisses me again, briefly. "Yes, milady, I do love you. I don't expect you to say it back. I need you to know, though. I can't let you escape again without knowing."

"Why?" It's the only thing I can think of to say. He still wants more? He loves me?

He furrows his brow, looking at me intently. "Why do I love you? That's your question. Are you serious?"

Of course, I'm serious. "Yes. Why? Why do you love me? How do you even know?"

"I love you because you're brilliant. Though I gotta say your brilliance isn't exactly shining very brightly lately." His voice is teasing. He winks at me.

"Eugene…" I warn.

He grins. Then he continues, "I love you for your fight. Your strength. Your compassion. You're fun. You make me laugh. You're beautiful. You are so brave. You inspire me every day."

I'm an inspiration? Ha. "Eugene, I'm a hot mess right now."

"I know." He absently runs his hand up and down my back.

I frown. *Would it kill him to argue this point?* "You know?!"

"If anything, it makes me love you more." He shrugs.

I open my mouth to say something, but the words get stuck.

Eugene continues, "I know I love you because when I hear your voice peace calms my very soul and I feel like I can face anything. When you are here with me, I feel whole. I feel like I'm home. So, yeah. That's how I know I love you."

I blink away tears. His love is so freely given and so undeserved. *I nearly threw this away.* "When I'm with you, I feel like I'm home. I feel that way, too. Nowhere else feels like home."

Eugene smiles at me. I could get used to seeing that smile on a regular basis. I continue hesitantly, "So I think, I maybe, love you, too."

Eugene has the audacity to laugh. Again. I give him a look of feigned hurt, but he doesn't buy it. He pulls me closer and whispers in my ear, repeating my words. "'I think, I maybe, love you, too?' That's what you're going with right now?"

"Uh, yes?" I wonder if he knows that his whispering in my ear is my kryptonite.

He laughs again. It's the best sound, even if it is at my expense. "Milady, that is something I can work with."

His grip around me tightens and he picks me up and spins us around. He puts me down and I look up at him and think to myself I was crazy to think the longing would ever go away. For the first time in maybe forever, I'm home.

His lips find mine again, no further interruptions from me. He deepens the kiss and I melt into his arms.

I am done.

Done with fighting my feelings for Eugene.

Done with avoiding any kind of relationship that is real.

Done with manipulating people for career advancement.

Done with all work and no play.

Done with bosses who take everything from me and leave me with nothing.

Done with a life that isn't worth living.

Done.

Epilogue

It's only been a few days since I met Eugene at his condo. I've already secured the HR Director position. The administration team was elated to have me back. I didn't even need a formal interview. Their excitement to have me back is the beginning of restoring my shattered confidence. I don't start for another several weeks, but I'm happy to have the time off. It's a significant pay cut, but it's still a good salary. More than that, it's a chance to have stability and a home. Set down roots.

Eugene decided he would open his own practice at the gym. He signed the paperwork this morning. The owner is ecstatic that he finally said yes - apparently she wanted Eugene to fill that role all along. Anyone else she'd interviewed didn't fit her expectations.

"I need to call my sister, I say. "If I'm in an actual relationship with someone, she's gonna be livid if she's not the first to know."

"Yeah, same with my sister, but I've got a better idea." He pulls out his phone and takes a picture of us together and sends it to his sister.

She immediately pings back.

> Is that your girl? I hope you aren't planning on letting her get away again. Too much moping last time.

"Was there moping?" I ask, teasing.

He shakes his head. "More than I care to admit."

He leans in to kiss me and snaps another pic. "There. That should satisfy her curiosity." He sends her the pic and then he sends it to me.

I forward it to Lily with the caption:

> The longing was always there. I'm gonna stay in Charleston...

Both sisters send about a million messages back and try to call. We, of course, ignore both of them.

At some point, I realize I'm starving. Eugene suggests going back to the BBQ place where we had dinner many months before.

We order lunch and sit down. I'm honest with him and admit I don't know how to navigate a real relationship. Or a job where I don't travel.

"I imagine it's like anything else, a day at a time. Besides, it's not like you can't handle anything thrown your way. You know, last time you had me here there was a proposal... do you have another?" His eyes twinkle with mischief.

I chuckle. "I remember. It was a *work* proposal. You seemed irritated by it."

"I was. I didn't want to talk about work. I wanted to be charming so you would fall for me."

"You were charming, I admit it. Smitten that early on, eh?"

"Of course. I was attracted to you the day we met, but that wasn't my fault. You were wearing your lucky black skirt."

"So my lucky black skirt did work? Without me climbing in your lap?" I say this while giggling. *When have I ever giggled?*

"I'm still annoyed that you didn't crawl in my lap like you do with your nerd tech guys."

I squeeze his hand. *That was a different life.* "I don't do that anymore."

Eugene smiles, then continues, "No, your lucky skirt didn't do me in. Not completely, anyway. After Mary told me how you stood up for her after the stapler incident. I was a goner. I fell hard. I have a weakness for strong women."

My mind drifts back to just before I left Charleston for New Orleans. "I was always attracted to you, but probably fell for you that day at Fort Sumter."

"That was a hard day for you, I'm sure. I knew you were mortified by the phone call with your idiot boss. When I hugged you goodbye I wanted so much to beg you to stay. With me. I should've told you then how I felt, but the timing felt off."

"I needed time to figure out some things. I needed time to realize that you weren't a fleeting attraction. You were someone worth keeping."

Eugene, because he is absolutely unable to stay serious for very long, he says "If you got any other proposals for me this time, I'm all ears. Like a marriage one, just for example."

"You don't think that's a bit fast?" I roll my eyes because I know he's joking. Mostly. He might be impulsive enough to go to the courthouse today. It's very odd because that thought does not make me panic. I cannot possibly imagine my life now without Eugene.

"I've been pining for you for months now. So it does not feel too fast to me, no." He says laughing. "I'm all in, milady. I want to spend the rest of my life with you. It's okay if you need time to catch up, I'm not going anywhere."

I point a French fry at him. "No proposals until you meet my sister, at least. Of course, she'll love you. I think she already does."

"Fine, you need to meet my sister, too. She does love you. I may have talked about you a good bit. Probably too much. She was furious - I do mean *furious* at me for letting you go off to New Orleans without trying to stop you. She's the reason I even agreed to let you come over when you first got to Charleston, you know."

This catches my attention. I raise my eyebrows.

"After you said you wanted to see me, I kind of freaked out. I had made the decision that I was done with you. I couldn't handle you coming in and out of my life."

"Eugene…"

He stops me from apologizing again. "It's okay. I understand now. She said I needed to hear you out. She convinced me to listen to your side of the story."

I clasp my hands together. "It's official. I love your sister. She's the greatest."

He laughs. We finish our food and go for a walk.

"Eugene, I've met so many healthcare providers who shared their stories with me. They trusted me with it. I wish there was a way I could help. Advocate for those of you who care for us when we need it most. Share your stories so that others could hear and maybe understand."

"Maybe you can. I know you're not going to be satisfied with a nine-to-five job. You're gonna need something more, even if it's just a side gig. Perhaps giving speeches to advocate for those of us in healthcare? A podcast or a book? I don't know. You'll figure it out, I'm here to support you, no matter what you decide."

He leans in to kiss me, but I blurt out, "Henrietta!"

"You have a bad habit of ill-timed name-blurting."

I give him a quick kiss and then say, "I need Henrietta. My nurse friend from New Orleans. We can do this together. A podcast that interviews healthcare workers. That spreads awareness. Advocates for their needs. She'd be great at the interviews. I wonder if she's still interested in moving to Charleston?"

Eugene searches my face for a moment before saying, "You look happy, milady. Not just because you're in my spectacular company." He winks here and grins ridiculously. *Of course he does.* "No, no - it's more than that, I think. It's like you seem at peace."

I am at peace. Maybe more so than I have ever been. I feel like I'm me again, except better. So much better.

I have a plan. Maybe I haven't found my way, but I am finding it. My priorities are aligned the right way this time.

Vivian Ashmead is back.

About the Author

I'm a physical therapist turned aspiring author. I've always loved writing and am excited to offer my debut novel, DONE.

Writing has been a much-needed escape into a fictional world, even if it's a world that mirrors real life.

I wrote DONE in the span of a year. I have 2 children and a day job. Writing was sporadic between my other responsibilities.

I'd find myself daydreaming about plot progression and character arcs. I've enjoyed creating the characters in my novel, I hope you will enjoy reading about them.

Thanks for checking out my debut novel, I hope it's the first of many more.